DON'T FOUL OUT!

DON'T FOUL OUT!

A Novel

Kenneth T. Ito

Best wishes!
Kenth J. Ito
6/16/04

iUniverse, Inc.
New York Lincoln Shanghai

Don't Foul Out!
A Novel

All Rights Reserved © 2004 by Kenneth T. Ito

iUniverse, Inc.

For information address:
iUniverse, Inc.
2021 Pine Lake Road, Suite 100
Lincoln, NE 68512
www.iuniverse.com

ISBN: 0-595-31357-4

Printed in the United States of America

To My Beloved Sister, Irene,
An Ardent Supporter of Education

May She Rest in Peace.

You can't depend on your eyes when your imagination is out of focus.

—Mark Twain

Contents

Acknowledgements

The author would like to express thanks to the following people for their help:

To Ken Kinoshita and Tim Soman for the book cover idea. Less is more, and I know we accomplished this feat because of your cleverness and creativity. And Tim, your craftsmanship and the execution of the idea are simply awesome. I know I was a pain!

To Christine, my sister, for giving me an assist with the names of the Spirits and always being around for me.

To Dad and Mom, and my amigos—Brad Amano, Ken Duer, Craig Nakata, Darryl Nakata and Don Spencer—for not laughing at me and supporting me when I said I was going to write a book.

To Marian Oshita and Joan Alvarado for the very insightful comments and creative criticisms on the numerous drafts that I wrote. I know it wasn't fun, but you gals definitely made the book that much better.

And lastly, to my Japanese language students at South High School, former and present, who inspired me to get off my "*oshiri*" to finally write this book. This is for all of you. Hope you read the book and get something out of it. Don't worry! I won't assign it as required reading. But, then again…

Thank you, thank you, and thank you! You've all helped me make my dream come true!

CHAPTER 1

What's Education Got to Do With It?

The pass was placed perfectly, but Eddie Holder, who was sitting in the bleachers, could tell it was too hard and too fast to handle. It zinged off the hands of the sandy-blonde haired player with freckles and bounced out of bounds just as the final buzzer sounded. And just like that, the game was over. The El Camino Matadors had faced its third defeat in a row.

Eddie looked around the gymnasium bitterly. The opposing visiting team danced and whooped, celebrating their victory, while the small home crowd mixed with teachers, parents and students silently and gloomily filed out of the gym.

Feeling the home crowd's disappointment, he pursed his lips as he took a look at the just recently installed scoreboard on the far wall of the gym. The scoreboard reading visitors, 72 and home, 71, he stared at it long and hard, hoping that the final results would change magically to his favor, but he knew in his heart that it would not.

Eddie Holder, a junior in high school, was a ruggedly handsome African-American, standing close to six feet three inches tall and weighing close to one hundred seventy pounds. Dressed in grunge with baggy blue jeans worn way below his waist and an oversized black t-shirt that came down past his hips, he had a well-shaped head that was shaven; a well-chiseled face; almond-shaped, gleaming brown eyes; a tall but broad nose; and a pierced left-ear. And when Eddie smiled, long dimples showed on either side of his face, radiating a feeling of warmth and friendliness. But tonight there would be neither dimples nor smiles from Eddie. Merely a huge frown.

Letting out a deep sigh, he pinched the bridge of his nose. Slowly, he turned his head from the scoreboard to observe the players on the home team—all with their heads hung low—drag themselves to the locker room, and he felt a tinge of guilt about the loss. Had he been on the floor, he would have easily caught that pass and laid the ball up and into the basket for the victory. Then again, the outcome of the game would have been decided by the middle of the first quarter, and the issue of this pathetic three game losing streak wouldn't be an issue. In fact, if Eddie Holder were healthy and playing, the Matadors would be undefeated.

Eddie got up from his seat, took another sigh and went down the bleachers. As he reached the bottom, he noticed that the sandy-blonde haired kid was underneath the basket with his head down, sobbing on his knees.

The kid's name was Richie Sykes. He was Eddie's replacement while Eddie rode the bench with an injury. Only a sophomore, he was just as tall as Eddie, but that was perhaps the only similarity. He was pale in complexion with freckles on his face and quite scrawny. Looking like he was raised in the mid-west on a farm, having this "aw, shucks" type of attitude, he didn't seem like an athlete. And to Eddie, at this particular moment, Richie wasn't one. If anything, he was a loser who didn't belong on the court, and as Eddie watched him sob from a far, he felt sheer satisfaction, knowing that Richie was feeling agony and guilt about the loss. It truly was Richie's fault that they had lost the game, and all the crying would not make up for that fact. Angry with Richie, Eddie wasn't about to offer any kind words to him.

Richie Sykes…there ain't no crying in basketball. Deal with it!

Eddie was about to yell and degrade him from across the court, but he noticed that one of the other players, Sam, a senior and the captain of the team, was walking over to talk to Richie.

Massive in height and weight, Sam was known for his relentless hustle on the boards and his brute force on the court, prompting names from the opponents like punisher or peewee-Shaq, but he was really the exact opposite when he stepped off the court. A young man of very few words, Sam generously volunteered his spare time—when he wasn't studying—working with underprivileged kids and helping his father out at the free clinic.

Sam put his arms around Richie's shoulders, and Eddie could see that he was offering words of wisdom, trying to console Richie. Always the big brother, Eddie thought to himself as he rolled his eyes.

As he continued to watch the two, he knew right away that Sam had said something to make Richie feel better. A faint smile appeared on Richie's face, and Sam patted him on the head encouragingly. Suddenly, the room felt suffocating with all this brotherly love and support, and Eddie began to feel a bit nauseous in the pit of his stomach. He definitely needed to get some fresh air.

Eddie knew that he would get his chance to criticize Richie later, so without saying a word, he slowly walked toward the open exit doors. Momentarily, he stopped at the door and eyed the two players having their little chat and then shrugged his shoulders as he left the gymnasium.

The cool night breeze from the ocean was usually a refreshing and calming influence for Eddie. More often than not, when he felt that he had had a bad practice or had done poorly on a test, which was becoming a common occurrence these days, he would often step out onto the balcony of his home and clear his head. The spectacular view of the Pacific Ocean from the balcony, particularly at sunset when the surface of the water shimmered a magnificent orange, also helped melt away any anxiety that Eddie felt that day. But tonight was a different story. The ocean breeze did nothing to take away the bitter taste left in Eddie's mouth from the loss. And what made matters worse was, as Eddie looked around the school campus, the students of El Camino didn't seem to be fazed by the loss at all. Most of them were hanging around laughing loudly, making plans to go the nearest Starbucks or pizza joint, and just having a good time.

It hurt Eddie deeply. How could these guys be so insensitive to the whole loss? Didn't the loss mean anything to them? They're acting like they don't even care, Eddie thought, as he walked by some of them to the nearest vending machines.

Eddie slipped a dollar into the slot of the machine and pressed the button for a bottle of water, but nothing came out. Agitatedly, he punched the change button a couple of times, but there was not even the rattling sound of change falling. This time he pressed the water button rapidly, and only the tinny electric buzz hummed from the machine.

"Great, just great," Eddie mumbled under his breath as he began to shake the machine forcefully. "First the game, now this?"

"Tough break, huh?" a voice said from behind.

Lowering his hands, Eddie turned around and addressed the man who spoke, "You talking about the game or this freakin' machine?"

The man, who was stout and balding, smiled at Eddie and shrugged his shoulders playfully. "Oh, I don't know. Maybe I was referring to the game, young Mr. Holder."

Recognizing the man, Eddie's eyes lit up. "Hey, you're Riley Johnson from the Daily Examiner. Whassup, man? How you doin'?"

"I'm doing fine," Riley Johnson said, "but I can't say much for this poor old defenseless machine."

Eddie scratched the top of his head embarrassedly. "Yeah…"

"So," Riley said as he pulled out a writing pad. "What's your take on tonight's game? You guys almost pulled it out."

"My take? Riley, ya know, if Eddie Holder was out there tonight, we would have kicked butt out there. Eddie Holder don't hold nothing back, and we always win."

"I see," Riley said, studying his writing pad. "So, how's the ankle of yours?"

"Got the doctor's okay to play the next game. And the Matadors will be winning again. I guarantee you. The Matadors need Eddie Holder."

"Uh-huh." Riley jotted something down in his pad quickly. "Hey, Ed, how about you and I go to the locker room and talk to the other guys. I want to hear how the other guys feel."

Eddie shrugged his broad shoulders. "No problem. Besides, I got a need to talk somebody. Let's go."

"Lead the way, my friend," Riley said as he gestured respectfully to Eddie. "Lead the way."

When the two of them stepped into the locker room, Eddie expected to see the guys moping around, but to his surprise, the mood of the locker room was similar to the one outside the gym. The players were anything but gloomy. They were joking with each other, while some sang in the showers. Eddie didn't like it one bit, and the feeling of anger and bitterness came roaring back. He wanted to reprimand them for losing the game, but he had other prey first: Richie Sykes.

Eddie spotted Richie, who was sitting on a bench near his locker, talking to Sam, and Flash, the starting point guard, and walked toward the group. Riley followed.

Before Eddie could light into Richie, Riley greeted, "Hey, Richie, Sam, Flash!" You guys remember me? Riley Johnson from the Daily Examiner."

Eddie would have to wait for his moment, as he stepped slightly away from the group and leaned against a locker casually.

Richie stood up and shook Riley's hand. "Yes, I do, sir."

Riley finished shaking hands with Richie and then shook Sam's hand. And then Flash.

Towering over the short writer for the local rag, Sam asked, "What's up, Riley?"

"Tough loss tonight." Riley looked down at his writing pad. "You know all you guys had really good games. It's not official, but, Sam, I think you had 12 points and 14 rebounds. Not bad for a guy who has no interest in pursuing basketball as a career."

"Thanks."

Riley turned to Richie. "You almost had the game winning shot there."

Richie sighed, "But I blew it."

"Ain't your fault, Richie," Flash chimed in. "My pass had too much zing-zing. I shoulda bounce-passed it to ya."

Richie smiled at his point guard. Like Sam, Flash was a senior. He was the only Japanese player on the team, and his real name was Ryūnosuke Shimabukuro. Ryūnosuke had emigrated to America only two years ago, but he already had a good command of the English language, picking up a lot of slang by hanging out with the guys and watching a lot of American television. With longish dyed brown hair—which seemed to be the norm these days in Japan—he had tried out for the team and turned out to be a deft ball handler with quick hands and great foot speed. And so, for this reason, but also because, quite simply, no one on the team could pronounce his name properly, he was appropriately dubbed "Flash" by his teammates.

"But still you guys never gave up, and that's wonderful," Riley said encouragingly. "When you guys made your 12-4 run in the last couple minutes of the game, did you know that Richie had eight of those twelve points and three of those baskets came on assists by Flash? You guys tried hard. You have nothing to be ashamed of."

"Thank you, sir," Richie said politely.

"Come on, call me Riley." Riley wanted to pat Richie on the shoulders, but since Richie was much taller, he had no choice but to pat his elbow awkwardly. "Now comes the hard part."

Richie raised an eyebrow. "Oh?"

"I have to ask these hard questions. It's part of the J.O.B."

Richie sighed deeply. "If you have to…"

Pulling out his pen from his back pocket, Riley asked bluntly, "What do you guys attribute to losing three straight games?"

Dead silence.

"The starting line-up is pretty much the same as last year except for Richie," Riley explained. "You only lost one game after a 3-3 start and made it to the city semi-finals. And yet, you're losing to some really weak teams this year. So, guys, what gives?"

"Riley, do you even have to ask a stupid question like that?" Eddie saw his opportunity and pounced on it like a predator attacking its prey.

Pushing off the locker, he took a couple of steps toward the group and gave them a cocky smirk. His whole mannerism conveyed pure confidence and arrogance.

"Right now our record is 2 wins and 3 losses. No biggie." Eddie shrugged his shoulders casually. "But Eddie Holder will be back in the starting line up next game, so we'll win the rest of them. It's dat simple."

"That's great news," Richie exclaimed. "So your ankle's all better now, Ed?"

Eddie spread his arms out wide. "Good as new, baby. Got the doctor's okay to practice tomorrow and everything."

Riley interrupted, "So, Eddie, what you're essentially saying is that you attribute the last three losses to your injury."

"You got that right," Eddie answered.

"That's an awfully bold statement to make." Riley frowned at Eddie.

"Ya see, Riles, we're like the Lakers. I'm the Shaq of the team. Without *moi*, we just so-so. But with Eddie Holder in the lineup, we dominate!" Eddie nodded his head toward Richie. "And if it wasn't for this retard screwing up here tonight, we'd be 3 and 2."

Eddie walked over to Richie and cruelly tapped his forehead a few times with his forefinger.

"Boy, what were you thinking when you dropped that pass outta bounds? Don't look like it was basketball to me. Eddie Holder coulda handled it and we would have won. Go back to the bench where you belong, sophomore."

Sam pulled Eddie away from Richie. "Enough, Eddie. Leave him alone."

Putting his hands up in surrender, Eddie backed away. "It's cool. Just wanted to make a point."

Eddie saluted the group and strolled away coolly to insult his other team-mates.

Out of concern for Richie, Riley looked over at him. "I'm sorry about that Richie. I'm sure he was just kidding."

Sam corrected, "Riley, he wasn't kidding. Eddie's different now. The beginning of last season he was just like Richie. 'Sir this, sir that. Yes, Mr. Johnson.' Remember?"

Riley nodded his head slightly. "Actually I do. What do you think changed him?"

"Oh, I don't know." Sam shrugged his huge shoulders, watching Eddie berate the other guys on the team at the far end of the locker room. "I guess after being the star of the team and then winning the MVP trophy last season, it went to his head."

"Yeah, now he got this big ol' watermelon head," Flash joked. "I just wish I could squash his head like a big zit and see all that puss come out."

Riley chuckled a little and then turned his attention back to Richie. "Well, you just keep your chin up, Richie. It's only one game. There's still a chance you guys can make the playoffs."

"Thank you, Mr. Johnson." Richie gave Riley a weak smile.

"Well, I'll let you guys hop to it," Riley said. "See you later."

"Yeah, see ya around, Riley," Sam said. "Hopefully you can interview us when Richie wins our next game."

Riley said, "That's the spirit, Sam."

And waving good-bye, he walked out of the locker room.

Eddie Holder entered his home quietly, and as he went up the stairs to his room, he heard his dad's deep soothing voice calling him from the living room. Eddie hopped back down a couple of steps and strolled into the huge living room that was decorated with some very tasteful and beautiful exotic African art. His dad and mom lay lazily on the leather couch listening to some jazz from a fully equipped entertainment system that was against one wall of the room. Eddie wasn't exactly sure what they were listening to, but he thought it might have been Miles Davis or that guy with the funny name, Dizzy Gillespie. To Eddie, jazz all sounded the same to him; rap was the only music for him.

"So, how was the game, son?" Eddie's dad, Earl, asked as Eddie sat on the floor next to the sofa.

"We sucked." Eddie's voice was slightly pitched because he was still agitated about the game.

"That's too bad," Dad said as he stroked his goatee speckled with gray hair. "How did Richie do tonight?"

Eddie rolled his eyes. "He's the one who blew it. It's all his fault. Man, if I didn't have this injury, we'd be undefeated."

Eddie's mom, Rachel, scolded her son. "Now, Eddie, that's not fair. I'm sure Richie did the best he could and so did the rest of the team. Besides, Eddie, haven't you more important things to worry about, like your history project?"

Again, Eddie rolled his eyes. "Mom, do we have to do this now?"

"You know, son," Dad interjected. "Your mother has a point. We've been very concerned about your grades since the beginning of the school year."

Waving his hand in dismissal, Eddie said coolly, "Chill out, pops. It's only temporary. I'll do better when basketball season ends."

"See, that's exactly my point." Dad got up from the sofa and went over to turn off the CD player.

From the entertainment system, he addressed Eddie somewhat sternly, "Son, I'm not against you playing basketball, but you have to be practical about it. Your grades last year were excellent, almost straight A's until you became a starter. And since then, your grades have plummeted dramatically, way below your ability. I regret not getting on you more, but you need to start hitting the books more seriously and pay less attention to basketball, young man."

Eddie looked at his mom for support, but she just nodded her head in agreement with her husband.

"Like I said, pops, I'll do better when the season's over."

"Well, you better," Mom said with a threatening tone. "We know that if you apply yourself, you're capable of anything. Eddie, you're a junior now, so you need to start thinking about college."

"College?" Eddie arched an eyebrow. He was about to protest, but trying to reason with his dad, who had an MBA degree and also a successful business, and his mom, who was a high school teacher, wouldn't serve any purpose. The best thing was to keep his mouth shut.

"Yes, college," Mom said.

With some quick thinking, Eddie lied to his parents, "I've been thinking about some universities like Duke or North Carolina. I'm pretty sure that I can get a basketball scholarship and get in."

Crossing his arms, Dad grunted disapprovingly, "So it comes to basketball."

"Pops, you know that Duke and North Carolina are good colleges. And they're not just known for basketball."

"But, as I know it, primarily basketball."

Eddie could feel that he was digging himself into a hole. "Just ideas, pops. Hey, I think Stanford and even UCLA would be cool schools."

Dad wagged his finger at Eddie. "Cool to you now, but maybe not so cool when you don't get accepted because of your grades. I wouldn't be counting too highly on getting a basketball scholarship so readily."

"Okay, pops, mom." Eddie knew that it was time to raise the white flag for now. "I will seriously concentrate on my studies."

"Good," Mom said as she clasped her hands together. "But you never did answer my question. What's your history project?"

Eddie faked a huge yawn and stretched his arms as he stood up. "Mom, I'll get back to you tomorrow. I'll think about it tonight and let you know."

"Good night, son," Dad said.

Mom gave Eddie a peck on the cheek. "Good night, Eddie."

After Eddie returned the kiss, he walked out of the living room and up the stairs. Rather than going directly to his own room, he stopped at the bedroom door of his little brother, Aaron. It was close to ten o'clock and past Aaron's bedtime, but Eddie knew that Aaron wasn't asleep. The lights were out from the looks of it, but he could hear the faint beeping sounds of a video game. Smiling to himself, Eddie pushed the door silently and went into the room.

"You best be asleep, boy!" Eddie said, imitating his father's voice.

In the dark, Eddie saw his little brother frantically covering himself with blankets and pretending to be asleep.

Eddie laughed aloud. "Hey, bro, it's only me…"

Aaron pushed the blankets away and sat up on the bed. "Aw, that sucks, Eddie!"

Eddie laughed again, sitting on the bed next to his little brother.

"You should be asleep," Eddie whispered.

Leaning back, Eddie felt something hard under the blankets. He knew exactly what it was. It was Aaron's Gameboy, and it was pretty obvious that Aaron had tried to hide it just as Eddie walked into the room.

Eddie stood up, turned on the lamp next to Aaron's bed and looked at his younger brother closely. Aaron was a chubby little boy of eight with huge round eyes and round cheeks. Sporting a flat top with a fade, Aaron had dimples like his older brother and a big goofy smile with buckteeth, which made him all the more adorable to Eddie.

"Pops would skin your hide if he knew you were playing videogames this late. You know the rules, right?"

"Yeah, Eddie, but you do it all the time."

"Sure, but I got different rules. I'm older." Eddie gave his younger brother a big, wide grin. "Besides, I don't get caught. Na mean?"

Aaron looked down and mumbled, "Ah, that's not fair. I wish I were you, Eddie."

"Soon enough, soon enough." Eddie patted Aaron's head gently.

"Hey, did you guys win?" Aaron asked innocently, looking up to his brother. Eddie frowned a bit. "Nah."

Aaron could feel his older brother's disappointment and gave him that goofy smile to make him feel better. Eddie smiled back and patted the top of Aaron's head gently again.

"Well, good night, little man," Eddie said. "See ya in the morning."

Eddie headed toward the door.

"Hey, Eddie," Aaron called.

"Yeah?"

"I'm sure you would've won if you played tonight."

"Yeah, I know. Good night," Eddie said as he left the room and closed the door.

Across the hall from Aaron's room was Eddie's room. The entire decor of the room was basketball. One wall had a framed and autographed Bulls jersey of Michael Jordan, while another wall had a framed poster of Magic Johnson passing a ball with his smooth patented style; the sliding closet doors were decorated with banners and stickers of various professional basketball teams. Eddie's desk facing the huge window was also cluttered with basketball memorabilia. Except for a single spiral notebook, there were no other schoolbooks on the desk.

Eddie entered and sat on his bed. He reached over to his desk and picked up the phone. He dialed a number, and the phone on the other end began to ring. After a third ring, someone picked up.

"Hello." The voice belonged to a girl, but the voice was quite raspy.

"How you doing, babe?" Eddie asked. "You feeling any better, Alicia?"

Alicia answered, "Barely, but I'll be back in school tomorrow because I have to take a biology exam. So, how was the game tonight?"

"Man, Richie Sykes messed up so bad." Picturing Richie dropping the ball out of bounds riled Eddie up all over again. "It's so whack I could kill that little punk."

"Geez, Eddie, don't be so hard on him. I'm sure he didn't do it on purpose."

"Well, you weren't there," Eddie said with agitation.

Alicia sighed on the phone. "I seem to remember a time when you were so..."

Eddie cut her off. "Hey, I just called to see how you were. So, I'll see you in school tomorrow, okay?"

"Sure. Hope you're in a better mood tomorrow." Alicia hung up the phone.

"Women!" Eddie muttered under his breath and lay on his bed.

Eddie didn't get it. Everybody seemed to be on Richie's side, and no one—not even his teammates—seemed bothered that he lost the game. But, tomorrow was another day, and Eddie knew that he would be back on the courts. He would will his team to win every game and make sure that Richie stayed permanently on the bench for the rest of the season. For all he cared, Richie Sykes could start for the team only after he graduated from high school.

It wasn't that Richie was a bad player or anything. In fact, Eddie knew that the boy had skills and acknowledged it secretly. What bothered Eddie the most was that—did he ever dare admit it in public—maybe Richie had too much raw talent and was a far superior player than Eddie was. And yet, Richie was too dumb to realize his own potential; basketball wasn't a priority with him, and he preferred to concentrate on other things such as the school newspaper, the yearbook staff and the chess club.

Chess club? Whadda waste of time!

Eddie shrugged his shoulders, knowing that he shouldn't dwell too much on Richie's priority because things would soon take their natural course and Eddie would be back playing on the team, winning games, and gathering all the praises he deserved in the community. He would win the city championship and be crowned the MVP again. *Who needs to study when I can have a have a great life playing basketball?* That thought alone comforted Eddie, and before long, he fell asleep, having grand dreams of a basketball career.

CHAPTER 2

Enter Slamm Dunkk

The white room was spotless and empty except for the sleek chrome desk and the chrome lamp that stood atop of it. Behind the desk, a man sat in a chair, looking at his computer monitor very intently. There was something extremely serious about this man, having deep set blue eyes, a permanent frown and deep creases on his forehead. He seemed to be "all-business and no play."

Impatiently, he looked at his watch. The dial read 1 minute past 9AM. He grunted to himself and shook his head disappointedly. This man had no tolerance for tardiness.

When he looked back at his monitor again, dazzling blue and yellow lights flickered suddenly for a few seconds in front of his desk, and a figure materialized.

"You're tardy once again," the man greeted the figure.

"Well, it's nice to see you, too, boss-man," the figure answered. "Besides, I'm only a minute late. You know how bad traffic is when you use the travel beam."

Grunting, the serious man examined the tall thin man whose clothing was a bizarre combination: White and purple hi-top basketball shoes, bright gold basketball warm-ups and a gold graduation cap. The get-up may have been a bit buffoonish, but the tall thin man was far from a clown. Very intellectual and trustworthy, he was the best of the best of his staff, so the boss could never really stay angry with the good-natured but sometimes tardy delegate for too long.

"Okay, Slamm Dunkk, let's get down to business."

Slamm Dunkk whistled. "What, no 'how are you, Slamm Dunkk? How's your mother, Slamm Dunkk?'"

The boss smiled ever so slightly. "Can we begin now?"

"Be my guest, boss-man."

The boss pressed a button on the command console on his desk, and the room instantly darkened. The wall opposite the desk transformed into a movie screen, projecting moving images of a young high school student playing basketball. Both Slamm Dunkk and the boss watched the brief film of the young man blocking shots, dunking over opponents and making some acrobatic shots a la Michael Jordan. When the film was over, only a still close-up shot of the young man remained on the screen even while the room returned to its normal lighting condition.

"Wow, that kid is really good." Slamm Dunkk whistled for the second time. "And he's a pretty handsome kid too, if I do say so myself."

As he pointed at the kid on the screen, the boss remarked, "And that kid is on a collision course to disaster."

Slamm Dunkk nodded his head knowingly. "I take it he's a wash-out academically."

"Not entirely, but he's headed that way, according to my informant."

"What's the kid's name?" Slamm Dunkk asked as he adjusted his cap.

"The name's Eddie Holder." Pulling open a drawer, the boss dragged out an extremely thick spiral notebook. The notebook was so heavy that he had to use both hands to hand it over to Slamm Dunkk.

Slamm Dunkk opened his eyes wide in disbelief. "Whoa! This is the file on the Holder kid? It's a new case, and you already have this much stuff?"

"Read it, study it and make your decisions."

"Sure, boss-man, I'll talk to your informant and scope out the situation with Eddie Holder. Maybe scare him a little to set him straight." Slamm Dunkk winked at the boss. "Who's my contact?"

"Riley," the boss answered. "He's extremely concerned about the kid."

"Gotcha, boss-man. I'm on the case."

The boss said, "Good luck."

Slamm Dunkk saluted his boss, and then in the same motion, he put a finger under his lower lip, chanting something softly. And similar to the way he appeared in the room, he disappeared with the same dazzling lights flickering on again. Only this time, he left billowy puffs of blue and yellow-colored smoke in his wake.

Fanning the smoke away unconcernedly, the boss mumbled to himself, "And this time, you're going to need a lot of it!"

"Okay, ladies," the coach said as his basketball team gathered around him. "We need to go through some fundamental drills today, but more importantly, we have to work on our conditioning and stamina."

All in unison, the team groaned.

"We were really close yesterday, but my feeling is that we would have won last night's game had we kept to our fundamentals and we weren't so tired at the end of the game."

"And you think that's the reason why we lost?" Eddie Holder asked. "Hey, you ask me, we lost because of Sykes. C'mon, coach, he choked."

At first, the coach took a peek at Richie, who was staring down at his feet unable to look at anybody, and then shifted his gaze to Eddie. "When we lose, we lose as a team. There shouldn't be any finger pointing at anyone."

"Whatever, coach." Eddie shrugged as if he didn't have a care in the world. "That's your opinion."

"Holder, zip it," the coach demanded. "If you don't like the way the team is run, then I suggest you find another sport."

Eddie gave the coach a smirk. "My bad."

"Fine." The coach continued to frown at Eddie. "No more finger pointing, okay? One for all and all for one. Remember that, because the next time I catch someone blaming another teammate for anything at all, he'll be kicked off the team. Is that understood?"

Everybody nodded heads agreeably except for Eddie, which the coach noticed but ignored. He'll have to have a talk with his star player about the attitude after practice.

"Okay, ladies, go out to the track and run a mile. Then we'll begin practice. I expect everybody back in less than fifteen."

Muttering to themselves, the team ran out of the gym collectively to do their mile.

As the coach waited for his team to come back, Riley Johnson entered the gymnasium with a younger man who stood almost a foot taller than he was. This younger man was none other than Slamm Dunkk, who wore jeans and a white tee shirt with a screen-printed photo of Albert Einstein on it. Below Einstein were the words, "A brilliant mind is a beautiful thing to waste."

"Hi ya, coach," Riley greeted. "This here is SD. He's new to the paper and I'm showing him the ropes. I've told him about Eddie Holder, and he wanted to come and see for himself."

"Nice to meet you." Slamm Dunkk shook the coach's hand. "Didn't you used to play college ball? Your team went all the way to the Sweet Sixteen."

The coach said, "Good memory, but that was about 20 years ago."

"You had the talent and could've gone pro. Why didn't you?"

A wide smile spread across the coach's face. "Oh, don't think I wasn't tempted, but it was always my dream to be a high school teacher and coach on the side."

"That's great. Not everybody does what they want to do in life."

"Thanks, SD," the coach said, "but you're awfully young to remember such an old timer like me. You can't be more than twenty-five years old."

"You'd be surprised, coach," Slamm Dunkk said with a wink. "Anyway, tell me a little bit about the team, especially this star of yours, Eddie Holder."

"Eddie's a great player. Let's see, he averaged close to 20 points and about 8 assists last year. Such a remarkable talent…"

"But?" Slamm Dunkk said.

The coach gave both Slamm Dunkk and Riley a sneer. "Well, ever since Eddie led the team to the playoffs last season and received all these rave reviews about how he has game, he's become determined to get even better and he doesn't care if he has to hurt others to do it. Anyway, that's my take on it. So right now, any more attention you give him will make him all the more cocky."

"Too bad," Slamm Dunkk said, shaking his head sadly. "Well, we'll just watch from the bleachers. And then Riley can make a decision about whether we should interview Eddie in the meantime. Right?"

"Sure, sounds okay to me, SD," Riley agreed, and both Slamm Dunkk and he took seats in the bleachers.

As they waited for the team to return, Slamm Dunkk said to Riley, "Things seem a bit tense here."

Riley nodded. "Well, the ball's in your court now, Slamm. My job is to inform. The rest is up to you. By the way, not that it's any of my business, but just how old are you wizards?"

"Correction, Spirit." Slamm Dunkk said, holding up a finger. "And to answer your question, let's just say I've been around since man first learned how to write with a pencil."

The players finally came back from their run, but most of them were per-spiring profusely, hunched over from exhaustion. The only ones who seemed to be holding it together were Eddie Holder and Flash.

"Hey, where's Richie and Sam?" the coach asked with concern. "They're usually the first ones back."

Taking a slight glance at Eddie, Flash answered, "Uh, Richie kinda had an accident, but cap is helping him out."

"I better go out there and take a look," the coach said with worry.

"Nah, it's cool, coach," Sam said aloud as he came jogging into the gym with Richie.

"You okay?" the coach asked as he ran over to Richie.

Richie smiled. "No problem, coach. I guess I was a bit clumsy and tripped over my own feet. I tweaked my ankle a little, but I'm fine."

"Good," the coach said. "We'll go through some drills, passing first and then a light scrimmage."

The guys took their positions and started the passing drills. Watching all of this quietly from the bleachers was a thoughtful Slamm Dunkk. Although Richie's fall seemed like just an accident, Slamm Dunkk smelled something fishy. He had no proof, but he knew something seemed a bit peculiar.

"Riley," Slamm Dunkk said in a whisper. "Did you notice how that one kid looked at Eddie first before he told the coach what happened?"

"Not really," Riley replied back. "Why?"

As he watched the drill on the court, Slamm Dunkk said, "Just being overly watchful, that's all."

The kids were split up into two groups of five, each group playing on both halves of the court according to their positions. The guards were in the high-post, above the key, while the two forwards and center were positioned in the low post. Eddie and Richie, both guards, were in the same group. Starting from the weak side of the court, the ball was passed in a clockwise fashion and kept going around until everyone had caught a pass. Then the motion would reverse and go counter-clockwise.

Eddie Holder found this drill really boring. He knew how to do chest passes and bounce passes. His skills were way beyond this elementary stuff. But if he belly-ached about how boring these drills were, he would get a mouth full from the coach, so he decided to spice up the drills a little bit. It didn't hurt that the player he was mainly passing to was Richie Sykes.

"A few more rounds of chest passes, then we go to bounce passes," the coach announced loudly.

Eddie Holder saw his chance. The moment he caught the pass from one of the forwards, he quickly rifled the ball from his chest, aiming at Richie's face. The pass was lightning quick and hard, but Richie caught the ball firmly with both of his strong hands, only inches from his face. Richie slowly brought the ball down, looking at Eddie over the top of the ball in mild shock; Eddie gave him a sly smile and nodded his head slightly.

"Hey, Sykes, you going to pass the ball?" the coach yelled out.

Reacting immediately, Richie threw a chest pass to the other forward.

"Hey, did you see that, Riley?" Slamm Dunkk said. "He threw that hard at his face on purpose."

"Told you he was a problem," Riley remarked plainly.

"I haven't had time to really study that dossier," Slamm Dunkk said regretfully. "Oh, man, he did it again!"

"Told you he was a problem," Riley said for the second time.

The drill reversed with the ball going in a clockwise direction. And now Richie was throwing chest passes to Eddie. Slamm Dunkk watched intently to see if Richie would get even, but he didn't. He simply passed the ball to Eddie as if nothing had happened.

"Normally, kids would strike back, but I guess Richie's different." Slamm Dunkk scratched his head in confusion. "I don't think it'll hurt if the tables got turned a bit."

Putting his forefingers together at the tips, Slamm Dunkk began to chant something softly to himself. Riley glanced at Slamm Dunkk briefly and then went back to watch the drills. Having seen some of these Spirits in action before, Riley knew more or less what to expect next.

Once Slamm Dunkk finished his chanting, he waved both of his hands toward Eddie's group and whispered, "Let it be done!"

Slamm Dunkk couldn't have timed it more perfectly. As soon as the words left his mouth, it was Richie's turn to pass the ball to Eddie. Richie zipped the pass from his chest, but the ball took a radical upward flight and flew over Eddie's head and bounced toward the far wall of the gym. Once it ricocheted off the wall, the ball went out the open door of the gym.

"What are you doing?" Eddie hollered at Richie. "What, first you can barely catch passes, and now you can't even throw passes right."

"Sorry, I guess it just slipped out of my hands." Richie said. "I'll get it if you want."

"Eddie Holder don't think so, man. He'll get it himself," Eddie said visibly upset.

Eddie ran out of the gym to retrieve the basketball, which was near the flagpole near the football bleachers. Sprinting to get it, Eddie tried to pick it up, but a deep monstrous voice from who knows where said unexpectedly, "I wouldn't do that if I were you."

Eddie glanced around, wondering where the voice came from. He didn't see anybody and shrugged to himself.

"Like I said, I wouldn't do it."

"Wud da?" Eddie turned his head to his left and then to his right frantically, and again he saw nobody around him. "It must be my imagination."

Eddie bent over to pick up the ball, but the basketball squeezed out of his hands and shot up, hovering in the air as if it were some orb floating in space. With his mouth wide open, Eddie looked at the floating basketball in astonishment. Then it happened without warning. Like some B-rated science fiction movie, the ball grew a huge mouth with razor sharp teeth and dove down to attack Eddie, ready to take an enormous bite out of him. With a big shriek, Eddie ducked down as the ball screeched over Eddie's head. The ball missed its initial target, and Eddie saw his chance to escape.

He quickly scrambled to the gym as fast as he could. He didn't know whether or not he would be safe if he reached the gym, but his teammates and coach were there. Maybe they wouldn't be able to help him at all, but at the very least, there was always safety in numbers.

When he ran, he looked to see where the basketball was, and to his dismay, the monster basketball was right behind him only a couple of inches away; however, now the basketball had grown four long thin legs as it gave hot pursuit. The ball tried to chomp Eddie's rear end, but with super fast reflexes, Eddie pulled his lower part of his body forward and shielded his rear end with his hands. With the gym being only a few more feet away, Eddie used the last of his energy to escape the deadly mouth of the monster basketball.

With his hands still covering his behind, Eddie burst into the gymnasium, screaming at the top of his lungs and ran toward the coach.

"Help me!" Eddie yelled. "It's after me!"

Immediately, all of Eddie's teammates stopped their basketball drills to see what Eddie was hollering about. They began to laugh and point at Eddie clutching his rear end as he ran and hid behind their coach.

"What's going on, Holder?" The coach was not amused.

Eddie screamed, "The ball attacked me! It had these huge teeth and long legs and tried to eat me!"

The coach sighed deeply. "Look, Holder, if this is your way of trying to get out of practice…"

"Coach, that basketball attacked Eddie Holder." Eddie was frantic as he pleaded with his coach. "I swear!"

"You mean this basketball?" Slamm Dunkk said as he approached both Eddie and the coach, while he spun the basketball expertly with the tip of his pinkie of his left hand.

"No, no, no. That ain't the basketball. This basketball had huge fangs and long legs. It came out of some horror movie but was even scarier!"

Eddie began to perspire with cold sweat. Was it all his imagination? It couldn't have been; it all seemed so real.

Slamm Dunkk examined the ball carefully. "This is the ball that rolled outside. It was just outside the door. Are you sure you're okay?"

Putting a hand on Eddie's shoulder, the coach scolded gently, "Look, I understand that this being your first day back and all, you want to make an impression. But this isn't the way to do it, Holder. You're just disrupting practice. Go home today and come back tomorrow with a better attitude."

"Honest, coach, that basketball attacked me," Eddie said, pointing frantically to the basketball Slamm Dunkk was spinning. "You have to believe Eddie Holder. Please!"

Behind him, his teammates roared in laughter. Flash was on the ground, holding his stomach because he was laughing so hard.

"Settle down, guys," the coach shouted. "If you don't, more laps."

Immediately the guys settled down, but there were still some muffled giggles as some of the players covered their mouths to stop from laughing aloud.

"Well, I tell you what," the coach said in a soft voice to Eddie. "Just hit the showers, and we'll talk about it tomorrow. Okay?"

"Alright, coach," Eddie said as he nodded his head a bit sadly and embarrassedly. "Eddie Holder will see you tomorrow."

As Eddie did an about face toward the lockers, the coach said, "And Eddie?"

Eddie turned his head. "Yeah, coach."

"Will you stop that Eddie Holder stuff? It's getting on my nerves."

"Yes," Eddie said absent-mindedly. "Eddie Holder will stop that."

The coach shook his head. "Just go."

With his head hung low, Eddie plodded gloomily to the locker room, and when he walked away from his teammates, he could feel them all chuckling and shaking their heads as if he were the village idiot.

In resignation, the coach shrugged his shoulders. And then he turned to Slamm Dunkk. "I don't know what's wrong with that kid. Well, at any rate, there's no interview today, SD. I'm sorry. Come back another day."

"Sure thing, coach," Slamm Dunkk said. "I guess it's a case of an overactive imagination."

"I don't know what it is. Now if you'll excuse me, I have a team to coach."

The coach walked to the center of the gymnasium to join his team, and both Slamm Dunkk and Riley walked out of the gym.

With a frown, Riley said, "Slamm, you think maybe you overdid it a bit. Eddie sure looked miserable. I mean, he's still a kid, you know."

Slamm Dunkk rubbed his chin. He did feel a little bit sorry for Eddie, but it was worth it. This was just the tip of the iceberg, and there was still a lot more to do.

"Maybe I did, but seeing what I saw today in the gym, the way he was treating that kid, Richie, Eddie deserved it. Besides, I don't think Eddie's going to give up basketball just because the ball tried to bite his butt off. He seems a much tougher hombre than that, and I doubt if this one thing is going to send him to the funny farm."

Shaking his head, Riley muttered, "I sure hope not, Slamm."

Slamm Dunkk had an amused expression on his face. "Well, look at it this way. If Eddie never holds another basketball again from today and devotes his time to his studies, then my job is done, isn't it?"

Riley nodded his head.

"But sadly, it's not going to be as simple as that." Slamm Dunkk shook Riley's hand. "Well, we'll be in touch."

Looking around the area and making sure that no one was watching, Slamm Dunkk chanted something under his breath. Dazzling lights of blue and yellow appearing out of nowhere surrounded him, and in a second, he disappeared, leaving a huge cloud of smoke behind.

Riley coughed as he brushed away the smoke. "Wow, talk about your second hand smoke…"

"Sorry!" Slamm Dunkk's voice echoed through the sky.

And Riley just laughed to himself as he walked off the school campus.

CHAPTER 3

A Monster is Born

Holding the Eddie Holder dossier in hand, Slamm Dunkk walked down the wide and long hallway of the wing known as Spirit Central. The hallway was busy with all sorts of Spirits discussing cases with each other or just running to get to their next appointment. He chuckled to himself as he waltzed by an extremely giant Spirit crouching down to hear the midget-sized Spirit talk in a very loud voice. If anything, Spirit Central was always an amusing place to be even if some of the cases were simple and boring. But Eddie Holder's case seemed nothing of the sort, and Slamm Dunkk knew he had to do some more research on the star jock who seemed to change from Dr. Jekyll to Mr. Hyde overnight without drinking any kind of formula.

At the far end of the hall, Slamm Dunkk opened the last door to his right and went down a long steep flight of stairs. The landing of the stairs offered a creaky old door that had a sign on it: "The Sorcery Arts Laboratory–Enter at own risk." Quietly, he opened the room. And as usual, it was dark, dank, silent and empty.

Unlike the sleek and modern conference rooms that were equipped with up-to-date hi-tech computers in the Spirit Central wing, the Sorcery Arts Laboratory was a direct contrast. The room was dimly lit, the only source of light coming from a single dim light bulb high above. The walls were built of dark granite, and there was no air flowing in or out of the room. In the center of the room was a huge black cauldron with some sort of reddish liquid that was boiling. Next to the cauldron was a single wooden table where there lay a musty old book of spells that was three times thicker than the size of Eddie Holder's dossier and double the size of a standard coffee table book. Aside from the cauldron and table, there was no other furniture.

Despite the room's simplicity, the Sorcery Arts Laboratory—although it didn't resemble any kind of laboratory—was an extremely important room with chock full of resources. Yet, more often than not, the laboratory was barely ever used.

It was truly a sad state of affairs, but unfortunately it was the sign of the times. A majority of the current and younger Spirits felt that "Sorcery Arts" was no longer a necessity and just simply too archaic of a system for their cases, so they chose not to move onto advanced "Spirit" training, of which "Sorcery Arts" was one of the main curriculum. Rather, once they completed their basic "Spirit" training or education, they leaped into the outside world and solved cases using state-of-the-art equipment without making any personal contact with the person they were trying to "save."

Slamm Dunkk likened this new breed of Spirits to young adults who went onto play professional ball right out of high school, and he didn't care for it too much. It wasn't that the young Spirits were by any means incompetent—they got the job done okay—but Slamm Dunkk strongly felt that by receiving advanced training, especially in "Sorcery Arts", it would only help them get a better understanding of the world and broaden their way of thinking.

There was really nothing Slamm Dunkk could do about the current situation. Nor could he worry about it. His job was to perform the best that he could to guide those people who needed help; Eddie Holder was one of those people in need right now although he didn't know it.

Slamm Dunkk placed the dossier on the table and opened the old spell book. Skimming through it, he found what he needed and then went to the cauldron, forming a triangle with his index fingers and thumbs over it.

Closing his eyes tightly, Slamm Dunkk chanted with a concentrated effort, "*Eddie Holder no kako ni modorareyoh. Eddie Holder no kako ni modorareyoh. Eddie Holder no kako ni modorareyoh...*"

A deep rumbling sound came from the cauldron, and then, suddenly, the red bubbling liquid erupted from the cauldron like lava from a volcano and shot up toward the high ceiling, changing into liquid that was psychedelic and vibrant. The liquid reached its peak and illuminated the once dim lab. And then, like a waterfall, the liquid cascaded over the chanting Slamm Dunkk and continued to do so until the lab was knee-deep in the liquid. The colorful liquid swished around a bit and settled in around Slamm Dunkk.

When the liquid became absolute still, Slamm Dunkk finally opened his eyes. But instead of the laboratory, Slamm Dunkk found himself in a high school auditorium full of students. In a semi-transparent state, he was hovering behind the podium of the stage, where the principal was addressing the students. It was apparent to Slamm Dunkk that this was some sort of assembly, and from his position, he could see everything that was going on, but no one else could see him.

The principal, a thin Hispanic man with a mustache, spoke into the microphone, "Before we begin our assembly, I wanted to announce our three students of the month. Our first student is Eddie Holder, a sophomore."

The students in the audience clapped politely, and there were a couple of whoops and hollers for Eddie.

"Say what?" Slamm Dunkk was thrown off-balance, almost falling on his rear end, but he quickly regained his balance. Curious and fascinated, he floated closer to the principal and examined the program that lay on top of the podium. The top of the program read, "Modern Dance Assembly, January 7th."

The principal continued on, "Eddie Holder is very deserving of this honor. Although he is a sophomore, he has a full load. He is a member of the varsity basketball team. At the same time, he does some volunteer work by mentoring some young students at the local recreation center. On top of that, he was on the honor roll this past quarter with 5 A's and 1 B. It is my pleasure to introduce Eddie Holder."

From the other side of the stage, Eddie appeared and walked over to the podium. To Slamm Dunkk, there was something about Eddie that seemed a bit different. Yes, he was a year younger, but that didn't seem to be it. Slamm Dunkk felt that this Eddie Holder from a year ago seemed less confident...No, that wasn't quite exactly it either...the confidence was there, but he was not full of himself like the present, brash Eddie Holder. In fact, this Eddie was much more mild-mannered and modest and quite dignified for a teenager.

With a soft voice, Eddie spoke into the microphone, "I just wanted to thank all my teachers for the support. It's because of their encouragement that I stand here today. And I also want to thank the coach and all my teammates, especially Flash and Sam, for helping me out on the court. I know that I'm the weak link on the team, but I'm so grateful that the coach has given me a chance to play for the team this year. Words can't express how appreciative I am. Finally, I want to thank my parents for always being around. Without them, I wouldn't be here to receive this award. Thank you."

The audience burst into applause. Slamm Dunkk, still standing behind the podium, saw that a couple of students, most likely teammates, stood up and hollered his name repeatedly.

Eddie said, "Thank you" once again and headed out toward the side of the stage.

Slamm Dunkk couldn't help but notice the happy tears in Eddie's eyes. He was genuinely filled with emotion and appreciative of receiving such a prestigious award, but what bothered Slamm Dunkk is how such a humble and sincere person could change into such a monster within a year. It just seemed unimaginable…But now, Slamm Dunkk realized just how much more research he had to do on Eddie. He couldn't just scratch the surface; he really had to dig deep to understand how the current Eddie Holder had come to be.

Forming a triangle with his fingers once again, Slamm Dunkk began to chant. Colorful wisps of smoke emerged from his mouth and swirled around him. Before long, Slamm Dunkk vanished into thin air, leaving the school auditorium behind.

This time Slamm Dunkk found himself in a high school gymnasium full of cheering students. Hovering near one of the backboards of the basketball court, he took in the sight of the entire gymnasium and saw Eddie Holder in a huddle with his teammates listening to the coach. He quickly floated over to the huddle, so that he could get a better gauge on what was going on.

The coach was diagramming a play where Sam would get the ball from Flash in the low post and force his way to the hoop. Either he would make the basketball or the referees would call a foul.

"Look, guys," the coach bellowed over the loud crowd. "We're down by a point, but, Sam, if you make the basket, we win and go to 500, and this win may give us a chance to get to the playoffs. But even if we don't win this game, you guys should be proud because we gave the number one team a run for their money. Now go on out there and give it your best."

The buzzer sounded and the teams took their place. At half court, Eddie Holder passed the ball to Flash. Flash dribbled around the perimeter a bit and saw an opening. He whipped a pass to Sam, but something went wrong. The moment Sam received the pass he was triple-teamed. Sam looked to pass for an open man, but the defense was too tight, poking and swarming around him like bees. In a panic, he threw up a prayer.

When Sam launched the ball, Eddie Holder eyed the arc of the basketball and knew right away that the shot was barely going to hit the front of the rim.

Timing it exactly right, Eddie leaped up, pulling away from the man who was guarding him, and grabbed the basketball with both hands just as it clanged off the rim. With emphasis, he slammed it into the basket…just as the final buzzer sounded.

The high school crowd exploded with excitement, and Eddie's teammates jumped up and down, hugging each other. But Eddie was stunned with his mouth wide open. It just seemed all too unbelievable to Eddie that he made the winning shot to put his team even at 3 wins and 3 losses.

Sam came up behind Eddie and hoisted him up into the air. Then his teammates surrounded them and began to scream excitedly, "Eddie, Eddie, Eddie…"

Turning red from embarrassment, Eddie yelled at the guys good-naturedly, "Cut it out, guys! It's no big deal."

"*Yatta! Yatta!*" Flash yelled out in Japanese. "You the man!"

His other teammates joined in, pointing at him, "Yeah, you're the man. We're gonna call you Big Game Ed!"

Shrugging his shoulders, Eddie allowed himself to enjoy the moment. Although it was still a bit uncomfortable, he let his screaming teammates carry him all the way to the locker room.

As Slamm Dunkk witnessed all of this, he realized that it was this single winning shot that was the turning point in Eddie Holder's life. Slamm Dunkk figured the team probably made a bigger deal out of it than it should have. The entire student body was probably guilty of it as well, and it was all this excitement that no doubt triggered the transformation of the once humble and likable Eddie Holder into an overly confident and despicable character.

Sadly, Slamm Dunkk shook his head. He now had an idea what incident had changed Eddie, and he would have to further study Eddie's dossier to understand the entire scope of it all. But even if he didn't have the full picture quite yet, Slamm Dunkk already knew that he had his work cut out for him.

Slamm Dunkk was back in the laboratory. He sat quietly, studying the dossier. Before that January 15th game, Eddie was your typical honor student, always putting forward a 110% percent effort in all subjects, but after that game, his grades started suffering. Whereas Eddie Holder was once a top student at the beginning of his sophomore year, he received all "C's" except for physical education by the end of school year. Not only that, Eddie Holder had quit the other clubs as well as his volunteer work at the center. It would seem that basketball had taken over Eddie Holder's world.

At the beginning of Eddie's junior year—the current school year—Slamm Dunkk found that Eddie had made no remarkable comebacks. He was still an average student, and worse yet, he received a "D" in trigonometry for a quarter grade.

Sighing deeply, Slamm Dunkk said to himself, "From honor student to slobber student…what a waste."

After studying the academic section of the dossier, Slamm Dunkk examined Eddie's vital stats for all his basketball games. There were plenty of detailed notes and newspaper clippings that accompanied the stats, and the more Slamm Dunkk read the stats, notes and newspaper articles, the more he frowned.

Before the January 15th game, Eddie was on the bench for the pre-season as well as the first four games. The stats listed that Eddie only got to start when the senior starting two-guard had a season ending injury. In the first four games, Eddie only played occasionally, averaging 2 points with 2 assists. But Eddie was made a full-time starter after the injury to the senior, and his scoring and rebounding increased every game. For the last 8 games of the season, Eddie's scoring average soared close to 20 points and his rebounding was about 8 per game. However, it wasn't the increased scoring and rebounding that Slamm Dunkk caught his eye; it was Eddie's assist statistic per game. Eddie's assist average was down each game. During the January 18th game, Eddie had a total of 8 assists, and in the next two games—the 7th and 8th game of the season—he had 8 and 7 assists respectively. In the 9th game, Eddie Holder had a monster game, but they had lost by one point.

There was a newspaper editorial from the high school newspaper on the 9th game that was paper-clipped to the dossier. The title of the article, "The Party is Over" caught Slamm Dunkk's attention, and he read through it very carefully:

The party is over, it would seem. Led by the emergence of the sudden all-star, Eddie Holder, the Matadors lost to Southwest High's Spartans by one point after a 3-game winning streak. Normally, this writer wouldn't make a big deal about losing a game, but it was what happened right after the game that became the impetus for writing this article.

After Sam Montgomery missed the last free throw that would have tied the game, Eddie Holder grabbed him by the shoulder and began shouting at him. Now this writer was an eyewitness to the whole thing, but unfortunately since this is a high school newspaper, I can't write verbatim what Holder shouted. I can only say there were some female dog references made more than a couple of times

To make matters worse, Holder, a sophomore and first year player on the varsity, put a hand to his neck and faked coughing, suggesting that Sam had choked at the line. Montgomery, a junior, began yelling back, and soon the two were ready to get into fisticuffs. Thank goodness the coach and some players were around to separate them. Sam seemed under control when a couple of the players held him back, but Eddie kept yelling and pointing at Sam, blaming him for their loss.

When asking the coach what had happened, he explained, "This happens all the time. Everybody wants to win, and tensions mount. Unfortunately, Mr. Holder took it to the extreme and took it out on Mr. Montgomery, but we had a team meeting, and everything should be okay. Mr. Holder and Mr. Montgomery have made their amends."

Sam Montgomery also had the same sentiment as his coach. "We're fine. Eddie and I had a long talk and we're cool. This won't happen again because I won't miss any more free throws, and that's a promise. We'll start our winning ways again."

Unfortunately, this writer had to take it a step further and went to talk to Holder, who was the instigator of the whole ordeal. Sorry to say, his stance was the complete opposite.

"He just choked. We just can't have that," Eddie Holder said, still livid over the loss. "If we're going to start winning, then Eddie Holder is going to have to start touching the ball more. If Eddie Holder gets the ball, the Matadors win. End of story."

When Holder was told by this writer that there was no "I" in team, he responded with, "But there's a 'me' somewhere in there."

Slamm Dunkk was thoroughly disgusted as he read the article and got the sinking feeling it wasn't going to get better. He continued to study the stat sheets, and just as he assumed, it was getting worse. From the 10th game and on, Eddie stopped sharing the ball altogether. Through the 10th and 12th game, Eddie averaged only 0.67 assists a game, and in the last two games of the season and the three-playoff games, the stat column had big fat zeroes all the way down. Eddie had obviously become a selfish player; he took it upon himself to win games and didn't trust his teammates. In fact, Eddie had 34 points in the semi-final game, which the Matadors lost, and it accounted for more than half of his team's point total.

Slamm Dunkk flipped through the dossier to see if there was any more important information on Eddie Holder, and he came to an interesting photograph, courtesy of the high school newspaper. The photograph taken after the loss in the semi-final game was of Flash and Sam with their heads down walking toward the locker room in the foreground. But it was what was in the background that leaped out at Slamm Dunkk. In the background of the photo, Eddie Holder was talking to a fat middle-aged man.

Slamm Dunkk was fairly sure he knew who the man was, but he wanted to be absolutely sure. He put his hand over the area of Eddie Holder and the man talking, and he chanted softly. The photo began to glow, and then two separate spheres of light came shooting out from under his hand and flew around the room. The spheres of light collided like two missiles exploding into each other in mid-air and slowly formed into two ghostly holograms of Eddie Holder and the fat middle-aged man.

The fat middle-aged man said, "Great game, Eddie. What, 33 points and 10 boards?"

"34 points, but who's counting?" Eddie said arrogantly as he shook the man's hand. "And who are you?"

The man gave Eddie his business card. "Here's my card. I think you can go pro, and that's my specialty. Let's talk again when the season starts up next year."

With that said, the two holograms faded off, and for about the hundredth time today, Slamm Dunkk shook his head in displeasure. He knew who this man was, and it wasn't good news. This man was none other than Herbert Waters or, in the Spirit circle, Shark Waters.

Formerly a student who was expelled from the Spirits Academy, the same institution that Slamm Dunkk had attended, Shark was an evil free-lance Spirit who had skills in the Sorcery Arts. He was known as an "absorber," and he preyed on weak-minded, innocent kids who had dreams of playing professionally but didn't have the talent to make it. His *modus operandi* was quite simple: Once in contact with his victims, Shark got into his victims' heads and gradually "absorbed" parts of their souls by first gaining their confidence and then tricking them into believing that he could make their dreams become a reality although he truly had no intention of helping them from the get-go. And if needed, he would use whatever Sorcery Arts skills he had to drive across his point and fully gain control of his victim's soul. A man with no morals whatsoever, his only aim was to make money and loads of it, and once he reached his goal, he deserted his unsuspecting victim, desperate and ruined, only to reappear again to claim another prey in a different identity.

Although Slamm Dunkk had never tangled with Shark in the past, he knew that some of his fellow Spirits had previously and lost, unable to save countless of souls that Shark absorbed. Slamm Dunkk rubbed his chin thoughtfully as he looked back again at the photo in the dossier. With this new piece of information involving Shark, Eddie's case was certainly a lot more serious than it looked. If Waters had approached Eddie once, chances were that he would approach him again. Slamm Dunkk knew that if he took the wrong step with Eddie, Shark would emerge victorious again. He had to carefully plan things out in order to right the wrong. He would have to call in the very best Spirits for help, but if that didn't work, then what?

Eddie was not happy, to say the least. At first, he felt humiliated because of what had happened, but the more he thought about it, the humiliation changed to anger. With his hands behind his head, he lay on his bed furiously, staring up at the ceiling. Maybe it was a bit silly that a man-eating basketball had scared the pants off of him, but who did his teammates think they were, laughing at him like that? *I'm the star of the team!* He had carried them last season, and if it weren't for his injury, they would be on top of the league this season, but they were in—what?—third place without him. He was the Tim Duncan of his team. They needed him so desperately, and yet, here they were ridiculing him. If anything, they should have supported him. *What ingrates! What a buncha retards!* He would show them that they had no right to laugh at him.

"Eddie," Mom said from behind the closed door.

Eddie got up and opened the door. "Yeah, ma?"

"Everything okay?" Eddie's mom asked in concern. "You've been so quiet."

Eddie paused for a minute. There was no way that he was going to tell his mom what had happened at practice. It was too unbelievable and embarrassing.

Giving his mom a big smile, Eddie said, "Yeah, mom, I'm okay. Just a bit tired from the first day of practice, but I've been concentrating on that project."

"Good for you, Eddie." Mom clapped her hands together in glee. "Well, there's a phone call for you downstairs."

"Who is it?"

She shrugged her shoulders. "A Mr. Herbert Waters. Said he was connected with the school basketball program."

"Waters? Hmm…I don't…" Eddie thought hard for a minute and then finally remembered Herbert Waters. "Oh, yeah, now I remember. He's not exactly a coach, but he is connected to the program."

"Well, don't keep him waiting. You can pick up the phone in our room."

"Thanks, mom," Eddie said as he raced to his parents' bedroom.

"And Eddie," Eddie's mom said.

Eddie stopped and turned around. "Yeah, mom?"

"I'm proud of you for at least thinking about your project."

"Sure thing, mom." Eddie ran into his parents' bedroom to pick up the phone. He felt a bit guilty about lying to his mom about "starting" on the project, but he figured he could lie his way through again if his mom or dad questioned him about what he decided to do his project on.

"Hello, Mr. Waters," Eddie spoke brightly into the receiver. "This is Eddie Holder."

"So you remember me?"

"Of course, Eddie Holder does." Eddie smiled to himself. "You're that agent guy who talked to Eddie Holder after that last game we lost."

Mr. Waters whistled. "I like that."

"What's that, sir?"

"The way you refer to yourself as Eddie Holder," Waters said. "It shows spunk and guts, but that's not what I wanted to talk to you about today. I apologize for not getting back to you sooner, you know, what with looking at other potential talent. But, Eddie Holder the man has always been on my mind. How are you doing, Eddie? How's that injury of yours?"

"Eddie Holder is back in practice, and he's pretty sure the coach will let him start the next game." Eddie wasn't really sure if it was true, but he felt like he had to talk himself up to Waters. "Yeah, Eddie Holder is positive about that. The team needs Eddie Holder."

"Nice to know that you haven't lost any of that confidence of yours. You know, after an injury, it's hard to get back into the groove."

"Yeah, I know," Eddie said, recalling the horrible man-eating basketball but immediately shaking it off. "So, what can Eddie Holder do for you, Mr. Waters?"

"You know we had that very brief discussion right after your loss in the semi-finals last season."

"Yeah." Eddie's heart began to beat rapidly with excitement.

"Well, you had just a sensational game that night, and I just can't forget it." Shark Waters smiled widely to himself. *Just pour it on, and reel the little sucker in!* "It's too bad that your teammates didn't help you, but I know talent when I see it. You polish that raw talent of yours and you can easily make the pros."

These were the exact words that Eddie wanted to hear. It was definitely more fuel to feed his already huge ego.

"Well, I want to meet you sometime over the weekend, that is, if you're interested."

Who wouldn't be?

"Of course, Eddie Holder is interested. Eddie Holder wants to go pro." Eddie yelled with excitement.

"Well then, I'm the man to make your dreams come true!" *Using words like "dreams come true" and "professional" worked like a charm every time!* "Eddie, I really want to discuss this with you very soon because I know you have 'it'."

"Well, you know, our next game is the day after tomorrow. You gonna watch Eddie Holder shine?"

"I wouldn't miss it for the world. My future star player." Shark smiled to himself again. "I'll talk to you soon."

Eddie put the receiver back in its place and walked toward his room. All the bad things that had occurred during practice seemed to vanish totally from Eddie's mind. The phone call from Waters thrilled Eddie, and it reinforced Eddie's own suspicions that his skills were way beyond high school basketball. He had the talent and potential to become a professional, and he wasn't going to allow his teammates to spoil his dream by losing more games. He would score every point if he had to, and show everyone—if they weren't convinced already—that he had the skills to be the next Kevin Garnett, perhaps even better…

CHAPTER 4

"Allow Me to Formally Introduce Myself..."

That night Eddie kept tossing and turning in his bed. He was so excited about his phone call from Waters and the prospect of being a superstar in the pros that he couldn't fall asleep. He knew that he should be working on his project, but somehow or another, all of his schoolwork had lost all the importance it once had at one time not so long ago.

Turning on the reading light next to him, he checked to see what time it was. The clock read half past one. He needed to get some sleep. Maybe a little bedtime reading would help.

Eddie reached over for a magazine that showcased on its cover past and present players of the famed Boston Celtics such as Bob Cousy, Bill Russell, John Havlicek, Larry Bird, Robert Parish, Kevin McHale, and Paul Pierce. This was Eddie's favorite issue, and he must have read it more than a dozen times, memorizing not only the exact location of the Celtics article but pretty much the entire issue.

He flipped through the pages and came to page 15 where the Celtics article should have been. But it was nowhere in sight. What he saw was an article on professional basketball players talking about the merits of an education. There were a couple of photos of players like Shaquille O'Neal and Vince Carter in their caps and gowns at their graduation ceremonies. Quickly, Eddie went to the table of contents, but there was no mention of the Celtics, which was extremely odd.

Eddie was certain that he had grabbed the right issue. But to be absolutely sure, he looked at the cover again. To his surprise and dismay, there were no pictures of the Boston Celtics players whatsoever. The cover was now of some player unknown to Eddie. Yet, for some reason, the player's face seemed vaguely familiar and Eddie couldn't figure out why. The player on the cover was dressed like some sort of goofy looking cartoon character wearing a cap and gown as he went up for a slam-dunk. In captions below the player were the words, "How Important Is Education to You?"

Eddie couldn't recall ever having bought this issue, and he really didn't want to read this magazine with the geeky looking player on it at this particular time, so he tossed it aside. What he really wanted to read was the article on the Celtics for the umpteenth time, so he rifled through a big pile of basketball magazines stacked neatly on his desk but didn't find the magazine that he wanted. Perhaps Aaron, who was a big Paul Pierce fan, had borrowed the magazine. Eddie would have to ask him about it tomorrow.

Finally, giving up on his search, Eddie went back to his bed and decided to go to sleep. And just as he was about to fall in a deep sleep, a loud voice cried out, "Eddie Holder!"

Startled out of his wits, Eddie got up from the bed only to be blinded by the reading light flashing in his face. He closed his eyes, looking away, and shook his head to shake away the after effects from the bright light. When he opened them again slowly, he jumped back from fright, almost falling off the bed.

"No!" Eddie screamed, frozen in fear as the basketball creature came toward him menacingly. "This can't be happening to me again! Please, no!!!!"

"Okay, only if you say so," a voice said from behind the basketball creature.

"Wud da?" Eddie was astonished and relieved at the same time to see Slamm Dunkk pulling back the basketball creature that was connected to a number of strings. As it turned out, the creature wasn't real. It was only a marionette.

"Hello, Eddie, how ya doin'?" Slamm Dunkk said as he put aside the basketball creature.

Tonight Slamm Dunkk wore a gold graduation cap and a basketball uniform. On the uniform was a design of a book and a rolled up diploma on top of it.

Eddie was no longer frightened, but he was now furious for being ridiculed again. "I seen you somewhere before. Who are you and how'd you get into my room?"

Slamm Dunkk reached over for the magazine that Eddie tossed aside earlier and pointed at the photo of himself on the front cover.

Giving him a toothy grin, he said kindly, "Allow me to…"

Without any warning at all, Dad barged into the room. "What's going on here, Eddie?"

Eddie pointed at the strange man who had come into his room uninvited. "Call the cops, pops. This guy's trespassing."

Eddie's dad looked where his son was pointing. There was no one in the room except for Eddie.

"Bad dream, kiddo. Go back to sleep."

Eddie could see Slamm Dunkk rolling on the ground, laughing his head off. "But, pops, he's here. Look carefully."

Dad shook his head in disgust. "Has that darn rap music finally gone to your head? I told you to listen to some jazz! Joke is over, Eddie. Go back to bed, young man, before I call the doctor to have your head examined."

"But…"

"Go back to sleep now!"

Eddie slunk in defeat. "Okay, pops, whatever you say."

"Good night," Dad said as he closed the door.

The moment Dad left the room, Eddie shot a dirty look at Slamm Dunkk, who smiled wickedly as if he had won the lottery and was rubbing it into Eddie.

"Eddie Holder don't know how you tricked him, but that wasn't funny. Who are you, anyhow? And where'd you get that stupid looking uniform?"

Slamm Dunkk bowed. "My name is Slamm Dunkk, double 'M' and 'K'. I have come to show you the way."

"You sound like someone from one of them corny old sci-fi movies," Eddie said boldly. "'I have come to show you the way.' Give Eddie Holder a break, man. Eddie Holder knows his way, and that way is basketball."

Slamm Dunkk rolled his eyes. "So, we're back to that Eddie Holder stuff again. It's getting a bit old. Sounds pretty lame, if you ask me."

"You're lame, if you ask Eddie Holder. Like Eddie Holder said, Eddie Holder knows his way and he don't need help from nobody."

"Well, you definitely need help with your grammar," Slamm Dunkk commented sarcastically.

"Leave Eddie Holder alone. Get outta here, ya freak!"

"You think you're some hot-shot, huh?" Slamm Dunkk arched his eyebrows at the cool Eddie Holder. "Well, I'll tell you something, pal. The way you're headed, you won't even live to bounce another basketball again. You're headed for disaster with a capital D. You get me, amigo?"

"What planet you from? You wear this funky old looking uniform and break into Eddie Holder's room and start lecturing Eddie Holder. You ain't got a clue about nothin'."

Slamm Dunkk had his strategies all worked out. He knew that it would take a long time to get Eddie to see the light. Tonight's meeting was purely a "getting to know you" sort of thing, and Slamm Dunkk didn't like what he saw. He couldn't get worked up over this punk kid who had no respect for anybody and saw basketball as his only meal ticket.

Slamm Dunkk said gently, "You weren't always like this. You used to study and you were enthusiastic about learning and school. A likable guy…long time ago."

"Hey, that was the old Eddie Holder," Eddie said. "This is the real Eddie Holder, and if you don't like it, just go back to where you came from."

"Well, the real you is taking the wrong path."

"Wrong path? Man, you don't know jack." Eddie pulled the covers up around him. "Eddie Holder is tired of you, so he demands that you leave now. You can't help Eddie Holder. Besides, Eddie Holder has his own posse, and they're going to take him down—to use your gay words—the right path."

"Uh-huh…" Slamm Dunkk was not amused. "And I take your posse—and by the way, posse is used for a group of people, not one person—is Herbert Waters?"

"How you know that Eddie Holder is talking to the guy? No one knows that!"

Giving Eddie a huge Cheshire cat-like grin, Slamm Dunkk said mockingly, "Slamm Dunkk has his resources."

Eddie's voice grew a bit of defensive. "Eddie Holder don't know Mr. Waters too good yet, but Eddie Holder knows that he can trust Mr. Waters. Mr. Waters is going to help give Eddie Holder his fame and fortune. Eddie Holder can't trust no guy who dresses up like a retard."

"And if he ends up being a fraud?"

"You still don't get it, huh? You stupid or somethin'? If Mr. Waters can't help Eddie Holder, then there'll be tons of other guys who'll be looking at Eddie Holder. Eddie Holder's talent speaks for itself."

Yeah, and so does your mouth, Slamm Dunkk thought to himself.

"So, since Eddie Holder has his perfect game plan all set up, he don't need help from you. Besides, Eddie Holder knows this is just one bad dream. You can't be for real, especially with that whack uniform. Eddie Holder will get up tomorrow morning, knowing that this be one bad nightmare."

Slamm Dunkk had seen enough of Eddie Holder for tonight. He knew that Eddie's head was going to get bigger, and with Herbert Waters in the mix, the whole thing would get even nastier. Slamm Dunkk figured that once Waters spoke with Mr. Big Head here, Eddie would definitely start believing he didn't need an education although Eddie probably was leaning toward that direction already; his whole attitude seemed to imply it.

"Well, if you believe that this is all a dream, then I'll leave for now. But let me just tell you this. You won't know when and where, but I guarantee you—you'll not only see me again, but you'll be visited by other people who'll force you to see the light."

"Yeah, yeah, whatever, doofus." Eddie pulled the covers over himself again and went to bed.

For a second, Slamm Dunkk stood there, staring at the back of Eddie. He hated not having the last word, and he pretty much detested the way Eddie made a mess of the English language. These sorts of petty things wouldn't have bothered a bigger Spirit, but at that moment, Slamm Dunkk didn't feel like being so noble. He had to show Eddie whom he was dealing with. Under his breath, he mumbled some words and pointed his finger at the unknowing Eddie. A yellowish-blue beam shot out from his fingers and hit Eddie in the back. The beam slowly surrounded Eddie, forming a transparent bubble around him.

Eddie felt the sudden temperature change all around him and opened his eyes. All at once, he became terrified. He didn't know what to make of this peculiar, suffocating bubble. With horror in his eyes, he looked at Slamm Dunkk and screamed hysterically at him. But the bubble was soundproof. Slamm Dunkk, with a huge smile on his face, snapped his fingers, and Eddie disappeared along with the bubble.

Slamm Dunkk stood quietly, waiting for a few seconds. And then he heard furious pounding on the front door. The voice was very muffled, but Slamm Dunkk knew that it was Eddie, who was trying to get back in the house.

"I always win!" Slamm Dunkk snapped his fingers again and disappeared from Eddie's room, knowing there was still some unfinished business to be done tonight.

It was about two in morning, and Herbert Waters was at his desk in his cluttered and foul smelling office, surfing the net and eating a large pastrami sandwich. He figured that since he was close to catching one fish with the proper bait, why not look for more ignorant, naïve young high school students who thought they could make it professionally after high school. The net was the perfect place to find loads of information on high school athletes.

After a couple of minutes or so, Waters found something that might help him out. It was a personal web page of some geek who was paying tribute to former and current high school athletes.

"Some guys have so much time on their hands," he said aloud, "but this may work."

He reached over for his pastrami sandwich and took a huge bite into it. Some of the meat spilled on the front of his shirt and he simply flicked it off. Herbert Waters was never one for personal hygiene.

Waters looked back at his computer and realized the screen was absolutely blank. "Hey, what's going on?"

He hit the side of the monitor a couple of times, and then the computer came back alive miraculously. An image shimmied like a mirage in the desert on the screen and settled into place. On the screen was now a CG image of a man in a gold cap and gown sticking his tongue out at Waters.

"What the…hey, this isn't right," Water said aloud again.

The CG image said, "You sure talk to yourself a lot."

"What's going on here?" Waters almost fell off his chair. He was shocked that the CG guy had spoken to him.

"You don't remember me, do you?" the CG image said.

At a loss for words, all Waters could do was shake his head.

"Well, let me refresh your memory," the CG image said.

The CG image reached over and its arm physically came out of the monitor; grabbing the front of the Waters' shirt, it yanked him into the computer.

"Hey!" Waters screamed at the top of his lungs.

Cowering in fear, Waters had his hands over his head in a squatting position. He couldn't make heads or tails of what was happening. Either that was one heck of a potent pastrami or he was going crazy, but all of it seemed too real for Waters.

"Relax, buddy," the CG image said, looking down at the fearful Waters.

Hesitantly, Waters looked up at the CG image and then inspected his surroundings. There was nothing around them but blackness. It was as if they were inside a black hole.

"What are you going to do to me?" Waters cried.

"Nothing…yet, my friend."

The CG image squatted beside Waters and looked at him for a while. "Hey, you really don't remember me, do you?"

Waters shook his head, looking fearfully at the CG image.

"Slamm Dunkk," the CG image said dramatically, putting his hand on his heart. "I'm hurt that you don't remember me."

Waters stared at Slamm Dunkk carefully. It began to register in his memory banks. He recognized Slamm Dunkk as one of his classmates during his short-lived stint at the Academy.

"You…" Waters muttered.

"That's right, it is I," Slamm Dunkk said pleasantly and stood up while staring at Shark Waters. "You'll never get away with this, pal."

Finally realizing that this was just a harmless prank by a mindless Spirit, Shark Waters was no longer afraid. He stood up and came menacingly close to Slamm Dunkk's face.

"With what?"

"Tough talk for a guy who was so unsure of himself just seconds ago." Slamm gave Shark a severe look. "Well, I might as warn you now, buster. You stay away from Eddie Holder or else!"

"Or else what?" Shark crossed his arms and glared fearlessly at Slamm Dunkk. "What are you going to do, Mr. Good Two Shoes?"

"I will exile you from this dimension forever," Slamm Dunkk warned.

Waters smiled evilly. "The Elders will never go for that. Besides, it's against Spirit law."

"You never know. Times change." Slamm Dunkk said, hoping his words might scare Waters.

But they didn't.

"By the time you get permission from the Elders, Eddie Holder will be all mine, and there will be nothing you can do." Waters laughed wickedly. "Nothing at all."

Slamm Dunkk frowned. "I will stop you, if it's the last thing that I do."

"Promises, promises."

"Sharkie, old boy, don't get me angry. You may not like me now, but you definitely won't like me even more when I'm mad. So be smart and keep your dirty paws off Eddie Holder."

Slamm Dunkk gave Waters a big warm smile, snapped his fingers and vanished from the black hole.

Waters bellowed, "Just who do you think you are? You don't scare…"

In mid-sentence, Waters realized that he was all alone and looked around nervously.

"Umm…hey…how am I supposed to get out of here?"

CHAPTER 5

One Lie After Another

It was usual for the basketball team to sit around at their "reserved" lunch table and horse around. When they were on the winning streak last year and made it into the playoffs, the other students were always hanging around the table, acting cool and mainly kissing up to the players. However, this year was a different story altogether. The team had a losing record without Eddie Holder, and hardly anyone paid attention to the players. But it didn't seem to matter to the players. They were happy just hanging out and talking with each other. It was all about the camaraderie.

"Man, we really need to win tomorrow," Flash said. "Or we're gonna be 2 games below 500. That sucks. *Tsumaranee.*"

Leaning against a pole nearby, Sam agreed. "Yeah, that's true. We need to start winning again, but I'm not sure if we can do it without Eddie. By the way, where is that guy? Not that I care or anything."

Richie answered Sam's question. "Uh, probably with Alicia or something. He told me after Spanish, he needed to spend time with her."

"He actually spoke to you?"

"Barely." Richie shrugged his shoulders. "I asked him if he was going to hang out with us during lunch. He just shook his head at me and said curtly, 'Alicia.'"

"Curtly?" Flash said aloud. "Dawg, that's a college word."

Sam said, "Richie, don't get me wrong, but Eddie used to use words like that, and he was all polite and everything, never dissing anybody the way he does now. Hey, Flash, remember the day after we got to 500 last year?"

Recalling that day, Flash shook his head, laughing to himself. "Richie, you were probably hanging out in the library that day—you know, looking up those college words—but we got in big trouble."

"What happened?" Richie asked, his eyes wide with curiosity.

Flash spread his arms wide and explained to Richie, "We got so hyped up about the win, we got on top of the tables and started singing and dancing. You know that song, right? The one about being champions."

Sam shook his head while smiling widely. "*We Are the Champions.*"

"Yeah, that song," Flash said. "Anyways, we started singing that song and start getting crazy and stuff. And Eddie was too shy, so we pulled him up to the table and put him on our shoulders. You know, we kinda wanted to show our appreciation because he won the game and all. You shoulda seen him, dawg. He was all red-faced."

Flash continued his story, "The students started chanting, 'Eddie, Eddie.' Man, it was a lot of fun until the principal came, broke it all up and got mad at us for almost starting a riot."

"And, there was poor old Eddie trying to cover up for us, saying that we did it for him." Sam shook his head sadly. "Man, what happened to that Eddie?"

"He's learned the meaning of winning and wants to teach it to all of you, my homies!"

Sam, Flash and Richie turned to see a grinning Eddie Holder with a young beautiful girl with long straight hair.

"Hi, Richie," the girl said as she waved to him.

Richie blushed and mumbled, "Hi, Alicia."

Eddie turned to Alicia angrily. "Why you saying hello to this retard here? He ain't worth your time, honey."

"Stop it, Eddie." Alicia narrowed her big brown eyes and shot Eddie a mean expression. "You can stand to be nice to Richie."

"Yeah, Ed," Flash chimed in. "You and Eddie were major buds. What's your problem, dawg?"

Eddie pulled away from Alicia and put his hands up slightly. "What is this? Let's pick on Eddie Holder day? Hey, Eddie Holder is just trying to toughen up Sykes here. And if he can't hang, then he should go home to his momma."

"It's just mean, Ed, and you know it," Sam said softly. "Seems to me that you're afraid that Richie's got skills and he's better than you."

"Well, why don't you let him do his own talking?" Eddie came closer to Richie, his face only inches away. "Why don't you defend yourself, boy?"

Richie looked away without saying anything.

"Little retard can't fight his own battles?"

"Eddie, just stop it!" Alicia shouted.

"Oh, now a girl comes to the little sophomore's rescue. What a joke!"

"Just leave him alone, Eddie," Alicia cried out. "You don't need to do this."

Eddie took a sideward glance at Alicia and smirked at her. "What? You his momma now?"

"Show some respect!"

Without warning, Richie shoved his palm into Eddie's face hard, sending him backwards. Eddie tried to keep his balance but fell on his rear end. For just a second, he had the expression of "I don't know what hit me," and he looked up dumbfounded at the group.

"What happened to you, Eddie?" Richie stood over Eddie. "You used to be my main dude. I thought you were so cool."

Angrily, Eddie stood up and grabbed Richie by the front of his shirt. "Eddie Holder can smash you and will, you loser!"

Before anything more could happen, Sam stepped in between the two and whispered into Eddie's ear. "Chill out. Principal at 12:00."

Eddie backed down. "All chilled out. It's cool."

"Yeah," Richie said, still angry. "It's cool."

"No problem, man." Eddie was a bit embarrassed about getting hit by Richie. "Eddie Holder gots to go anyway. Alicia, you coming?"

Alicia shook her head no.

"Fine, don't need you anyway." Eddie looked back to Richie and winked at him. "Stay with your momma. And make sure she puts sticky stuff on your hands so you don't drop any balls out of bounds tomorrow."

Richie gave Eddie the meanest look he could muster up, but it didn't seem to faze Eddie at all.

"Well, guys, it's been fun. See ya, and Eddie Holder definitely don't wanna be ya." Getting in the last word, Eddie saluted the group, turned around and walked away.

The coach blew his whistle, and the basketball team huddled up around him. Eddie Holder with a very cool attitude stayed a couple of feet behind the group as he listened in.

"Okay, ladies," the coach said to his team. "I've been hearing stuff about what's been going on with you ladies. Look, I don't like what I'm hearing, and I have to stress to you that if we're going to start winning, we need to start working together. We can't fight with each other."

The coach shot a look at Eddie and then at Richie, who was standing in front of the coach.

Richie whispered, "Coach, I'm sorry. I guess I still feel bad about losing the game for us the other night and I lost my temper. It won't happen again."

"Make sure it doesn't, or you won't be starting any more games," the coach said. "Holder?"

"Yeah, whatever he said, coach." Eddie waved a hand at the coach.

"I want to hear an apology, Holder."

Eddie bit his tongue. He wanted to argue with the coach, but after what had happened yesterday with the man-eating basketball incident, he couldn't afford to act like a dude with attitude.

"Yeah, Eddie Holder is sorry," Eddie said half-heartedly to no one in particular.

"Okay," the coach said, letting Eddie's insincere apology slide. "Now, ladies, we have a lot of work to do before Friday's game. I brought in someone who can help us throughout the season. He has a really busy schedule, but he's agreed to help us out. He's a really good friend of mine."

"Who is he, coach?" Flash asked.

"You'll see in just a sec." The coach turned toward the doorway to the lockers and yelled out, "It's your cue!"

From the doorway, a mountain of a man came jogging out toward the group of antsy basketball players. An African-American, every single aspect of the man was muscular: his strong neck, his beefy arms and legs, his broad shoulders, and his huge barrel of a chest. But it wasn't just his physical features that stood out. His whole existence was bigger than life itself, exhibiting so much magnificent strength and wisdom, that had a black bear been standing next to him, the black bear would have literally bowed down to him with the deepest respect.

The huge African-American stood in front of the group, his arms crossed and a grimace on his face. The players just stared back, a bit awed at the size of the man.

"You think they're going to scrimmage, or are they going to stand there all day long like deer in headlights?" Even the large man's gravelly voice had force.

Sam cautiously stepped forward and pointed at the older man. He stuttered, "Hey, I know you...you're Byron Thompson!"

Flash said, "Who?"

Turning back to the group, Sam was filled with excitement. "Guys, you don't know who this guy is? Byron Thompson...he's a legend in street ball tournaments! I've seen him play, and he's so awesome. He'd give Shaq a run for his money."

Sam looked back at Byron Thompson. "You played at Santa Clara, right?"

Byron gave a little smile and nodded his head. "That's right, son."

"Every time my dad and I watch basketball on the tube, my dad always brings you up. He said that you were a kick-butt college player. Your nickname was the Wizard. My dad went to a rival college or something. And every time they played you guys, you always had this monster game. Something like a triple double, 35 points, 15 rebounds, 10 blocks. Everybody at my dad's school hated you."

Byron gave a little laugh, but the normally reserved Sam rambled on, "My dad says you could have gone pro easily, drafted in the top ten at least, but he admires you all the more because you didn't make sports your career and became one of the top sports medicine surgeons in the country. And you're always helping out the community."

"Really? That's so cool!" Flash was excited now, and there was a little buzz among the players. "Hey, Mr. Thompson, how'd you get stuck with us? We're not like one of the top high schools in basketball, ya know?"

"Well," Bryon Thompson said with a smile on his face, enjoying the moment. "Your coach and I go back a long way. We'll have plenty of time to talk later. I don't want to waste any time, so what I want you guys to do is break up into two teams and have a scrimmage. I'll be watching all of you guys for your strengths and weaknesses. Try to give you some pointers."

The team broke up into two groups, but Sam was still standing in front of Byron, now with his mouth agape. Flash and Richie came to Sam, and Flash tapped Sam on the shoulder, but there was no response. It was as if Sam had been frozen by a snowstorm.

Richie laughed, "Hey, Cap, are you going to stand there all day long. You heard the man, let's go play some b-ball."

"Yo, dawg, anybody home?" Flash tapped on Sam's head lightly but still no response.

Byron barked out, "Come on, guy…you heard the guys, they're waiting."

Suddenly, Sam stood at attention like a soldier and saluted. "Yes, sir, right away, sir."

Then he about-faced and ran off with Richie and Flash to play some basketball.

The coach shrugged. "How come I could never get Sam to pay attention to me like that?"

Byron Thompson just chuckled loudly.

Byron and the coach watched the scrimmage carefully. The players were trying too hard to impress—maybe hot-dogging a little—and the scrimmage was very sloppy. There were easy baskets missed, a lot of traveling and turnovers by players. About the only player who shone above all of them was Eddie Holder, but he wasn't perfect as he too made some errors and some of his timing was off. This was, however, understandable, as this was his first full day of practice after a long injury.

"Like you said, that Holder kid is sharp, and he's got potential," Byron commented. "His timing is somewhat off, and the other criticism I have is he doesn't like to pass the ball too much. He sort of reminds me of somebody."

The coach scratched the top of the head. "The timing is off because he's been injured, and about the other thing…that's partially the reason why I wanted you to come here. Byron, Holder doesn't trust his teammates, and it's getting worse. I wanted you to talk to him about the importance of trust and team play. And you know all about team play."

"Well, I'll see what I can do." Byron smiled at the coach. "I'll try to set him straight."

The coach blew his whistle, the scrimmaging came to an end, and the players gathered around the coach and Byron Thompson.

"Ladies," the coach addressed his players, "that was some sloppy scrimmaging out there. I know you guys can do better. Maybe you can focus a lot more and put your best foot forward tomorrow during practice. Now go hit the showers."

Sam asked, "Okay, but will Mr. Thompson be here tomorrow to give us pointers?"

"Of course," Byron answered. "And it's Byron."

"Awesome!" Sam explained.

As the players shook hands with Byron, waving good-bye and heading toward the locker room, the coach called for Eddie.

"Yeah, coach." Eddie turned around. "Wud up?"

"Come back here. We need to talk a bit."

"Sure, no problem." Eddie shrugged. "Whatcha wanna to talk to Eddie Holder about?"

The coach shook his head but let the Eddie Holder reference slide. "We were watching you in scrimmage today. Not bad considering you haven't played in awhile."

"Thanks, coach, but Eddie Holder could do better if his teammates were..."

"Okay," the coach interrupted before Eddie could finish his sentence. "First off, when you talk to Byron and me, can you refer to yourself as 'I'. And before you finish your sentence, don't. I know what you're going to say."

Byron Thompson stepped forward and put his big hand on Eddie's shoulder. "You have all the potential in the world, but you need to trust your teammates. You need to distribute the ball a little more."

"Like Eddie Holder...I mean...like I said, my teammates can't finish their plays. It just don't feel right when I'm out there with them. It ain't my fault if you can't develop your players, coach. They can't play, so I gots to do my own thang."

"Right now, I don't want you to do your own thing," the coach started to shout, pointing at Eddie. "If you can't play with your teammates, I may have to..."

"Coach." Byron grabbed the coach's arm to calm him down. "Maybe it'll be better if I talk to Eddie alone."

Realizing he was yelling, the coach took a deep breath and said, "Okay, fine. When you're done, I'll be in the office. You take it from here."

The coach walked away.

Byron Thompson gave Eddie a wide grin. "Let's shoot some hoops."

Eddie and Byron Thompson were shooting around for a while, and Eddie thoroughly enjoyed the moment. It wasn't everyday that he got to shoot hoops with a former all-star collegiate. After their last game of horse, which the big guy won easily, they sat down on the bench to take a breath.

For awhile, the two were silent, taking in the view of the empty basketball court.

Byron finally said, "I think everybody on the team has potential, and so do you, Eddie. But you need to understand the concept of team play, and you also need to develop your fundamentals and skills. You can go a long way if you do that."

Thinking about what Herbert Waters had said a day earlier, Eddie asked, "Can I go professional?"

Byron looked seriously at Eddie. "How old are you, Eddie?"

"Sixteen, Bee."

"It's Byron. And in all honesty, you shouldn't even be thinking about that right now."

Eddie got up from the bench, picked up the ball and shot the ball twenty feet away from the basket. It clanged off the front of the rim.

Shrugging, Eddie looked toward Byron and said, "Why not? Man, everybody's going professional right after school. KG started it all. Then you got T-Mac and Jermaine O'Neal. And now, LeBron James."

Byron nodded thoughtfully. "Sure, but do you know how difficult it is to get into the pros right after high school or even during college? I tell you, I don't know how many times I thought about making myself eligible for the draft, but I knew that I wasn't ready. Maybe physically, but definitely not mentally."

Eddie pouted a bit at Byron.

"It's true, Ed," Byron said, shrugging his shoulders. "I had plenty of friends who went pro, but a lot of them didn't make it. They went overseas to play, and I didn't want to end up like them, so I chose to make basketball a hobby and make medicine my career. I knew better. I'm doing what I like, and I feel like I'm contributing something to our society. I'm not saying basketball isn't important, but there are more important things that you can do with your life."

Eddie shook his head. He didn't like the direction of the conversation.

"I watch you on the court, and I know that you have a lot of talent, but you need to grow up, not just physically but mentally as well. If you truly think that you have the talent and desire to become professional, then go for it. But just remember this. For every LeBron James, there are hundreds of others, maybe even thousands, who have failed. I guess what I'm saying is have a back-up plan if all else fails. Do you?"

Sadly, Eddie shook his head. He wanted to scream at Byron, but screaming wouldn't help his cause. Byron had his strong beliefs, but Eddie had his too. And he wasn't about to let this guy convince him to follow some other so-called loftier goal.

"What do your parents say?" Byron asked.

"Nothing, really." Eddie shrugged. "They just always say do your best in whatever you do.

It wasn't really a lie. His parents always encouraged him to do the best—even in basketball—but he knew they were dead set against him pursuing it professionally right after high school.

"You need to think about different options besides basketball. Like I said, you're still young yet, so look at other things. There's more to life than just basketball. Look at guys like Magic Johnson. Magic is a successful businessman and does so much for his community. Look at Shaquille O'Neal. He graduated from LSU, even while playing pro ball, and now he's saying he wants to pursue law enforcement after he retires."

Byron continued on, "You may not know him because he's way before your time and mine, but there's Bill Bradley. The man played pro ball, but he's a politician now. The bottom line is, basically, have a back-up plan. What happens if your basketball dreams don't pan out? You know, that is possible."

"Yes, sir." Eddie was thoroughly agitated now and turning red by the second. He knew that Byron was only trying to advise him, but to him, it sounded more like a sermon that was just preventing him from playing basketball.

Obviously noting that Eddie was perturbed, Byron said gently, "Look, I didn't mean to preach to you, but I just want you to make right and responsible decisions for yourself."

Taking in a deep breath, Eddie did all he could do to keep his temper in check. "No disrespect, Bee, but I can make the right decisions, and I don't need the people around me telling me what to do. It's more pressure on me."

Byron shrugged his massive shoulders. "Then do what you have to do, and hope that it comes out the way that you want. Ultimately, it's your choice."

The two of them were silent for a moment. Then Eddie said, "Can we play some more hoops? I want you to see more of my moves."

"Sure," Byron Thompson said disappointedly, realizing that his little lecture hadn't budged Eddie one bit in his thinking.

Eddie came home exhausted from practice. Dumping his backpack on the floor, he sat on the sofa, placed his feet on the coffee table and then turned on the wide screen television using the remote. The news came on, and immediately Eddie changed it to a sports channel.

Behind Eddie, his mom called, "Eddie, is that you?"

"Yeah, mom," Eddie muttered.

"Well, turn off the television. Dinner's about ready. And Eddie…"

"Yeah, mom?"

"Where are your manners? You don't greet your parents when you come home, and get your feet off the furniture."

Eddie sighed. He took his feet off the table, turning off the television and going into the kitchen. Mom was at the stove, pouring meat stew into a bowl from a huge pot.

Eddie said, "Hi, mom."

"That's better." Mom handed him two bowls, the one she had in her hand and the other one placed on the counter.

He gave her a peck on the cheek as he took the bowls and carried them to the dining room where Dad and Aaron were already eating their salads. Eddie placed the stew in front of Aaron, and then he pat the boy's head with his free hand. Aaron smiled at Eddie, and Eddie winked back as he went over to his father and placed the stew in front of his father.

Dad looked up. "Glad you decided to join us. How are you doing, son?"

"Okay," Eddie answered without energy, sitting next to his dad. "Practice was just okay, but some guy came by to help coach us. No big deal."

Eddie reached over for the Ranch salad dressing and drowned his salad with a huge big glob. And then he shoved a forkful of salad into his mouth hungrily, as if he hadn't eaten for days, and chewed eagerly with his mouth open.

Watching his older brother's every move closely since he entered the room, Aaron tried to imitate the way his older brother was eating by slurping his stew and chewing loudly.

Dad noticed how ill mannered both of his boys were and addressed it. "Boys, where are your manners?"

"Sorry, pops," Eddie said, shrugging his shoulders. "I guess I was hungrier than I thought."

Still copying big brother, Aaron shrugged his shoulders also. "Me, too."

Dad sighed a bit, looking at his younger son. Whatever Eddie did, Aaron was sure to follow suit. It was wonderful that there was such a strong bond between his two boys, but perhaps Aaron idolized his older brother a bit too much. At the same time, Dad realized, however, that it was just a phase that Aaron would grow out of eventually…hopefully.

Turning to Eddie, Dad asked, "So, who's this guy that has gotten you so enthusiastic?"

Eddie picked up on his dad's sarcasm and answered, "Just some guy who's really famous, at least according to Sam and his old man."

"So I'm supposed to guess who this guy is? The Rock? LL Cool J?"

Aaron laughed. "That's a good one, pops."

Also laughing, perking up a bit, Eddie responded, "Yeah, they came, too. Nah, pops, a guy named Byron Thompson. I shot around with him after practice. He said that I have potential."

"Isn't that wonderful, dear," Mom said as she came into the dining room and sat down.

"Eddie, why don't you tell us all about it," Dad said.

With his mouth full, Eddie exclaimed, "Man, you shoulda seen me on the courts with Mr. Thompson. I was all razzle-dazzle. Boy, did I give him a work-out."

"That's cool, Eddie!" Aaron said loudly.

"Eddie, don't talk with your mouth full," Mom scolded.

"But, mom, it's true," Eddie fibbed. "He couldn't keep up with me."

Dad shook his head. "That's great for you and I can understand your excitement, but listen to your mother. Mind your manners, son."

"What else did Mr. Thompson have to say?" Dad asked, hoping that it was more than just playing basketball.

Eddie looked down thoughtfully for a moment. He was still a bit upset about the lecture that Byron Thompson had given him, but he decided not to say anything about it to his parents.

"Well, not much else," Eddie lied. "Just talked mostly about how good I was."

Mom said with glee, "I'm glad you had a enjoyable time today, but, you know, you still have more important things to do like your history project. Have you decided on anything? You know it's due soon."

"There's plenty of time."

"Eddie!" Mom scolded.

"Mom, I can deal with homework later. Basketball's more important to me."

Dad cleared his throat. "Son, I thought we had this conversation before. Your studies come first."

"Oh, c'mon, pops." Eddie became flustered. "I'll start on my project after I shoot around a bit more after dinner."

"There will be no practice. You need to start your project after dinner," Dad demanded. "If I have to, I will take down that basketball hoop."

Eddie threw up his hands. "Whatever."

"No, it will not be whatever. You will do what we say. We know what's good for you."

Before Eddie could say anything back, the phone rang. Right away, Aaron announced that he would get it and ran into the kitchen. Then he came back and said the call was for Eddie.

As Eddie stood up to get the call, Dad said, "After dinner, we need to discuss this further. You're not taking your studies very seriously, and it's really affecting your life."

Eddie looked at his dad with a grim expression for a brief moment, shrugged his shoulders and then went to get his phone call.

"Hello?" Eddie spoke into the receiver.

"Hello, Mr. Young Eddie Holder."

"I'm sorry, who is this?"

"Hey, I'm surprised you don't recognize my voice. Herbert Waters here."

"Oh, hello, Mr. Waters," Eddie said pleasantly. "Sorry, Eddie Holder didn't recognize your voice. He has a lot of things on his mind."

"Call me, Herb. All of my friends do." Herbert's voice was filled with enthusiasm.

"Mr. Waters, now is not a good time to talk," Eddie whispered. "Can Eddie Holder call you back or something?"

"Oh, this won't take long. Give me a couple of seconds. And stop being so formal, Ed."

"Okay, sir."

Herbert laughed at Eddie's good manners. "Look, kid, we talked about the possibility of you going professional yesterday, but after thinking about it, I really want to discuss things with you sooner. You have a game tomorrow night, right? You think we can talk a little after the game?"

"I guess it'll be okay."

"Great, I'll meet you in front of the gym after the game."

"Okay, I'll see you then."

"And Eddie." There was a brief pause. "Don't mention this to your parents or coach until we've had our little discussion. Is that clear?"

"Yes, sir."

"Good. See you tomorrow night, then." Shark Waters hung up the phone.

Eddie put the receiver back and returned to the dining room.

"Who was that?" Mom asked.

As Eddie sat, he lied flatly, "Sam. He wanted to make sure we were on for this Saturday."

Aaron glanced at his older brother. He knew it wasn't Sam, but he didn't say anything. His older brother must have had his reasons for lying, and he wasn't about to tattle on Eddie.

Dad said, "Well, you won't be if you don't start picking up the books, young man."

"Just chill out, pops." Eddie threw up his hands. "Why can't you understand how important basketball is to me? It's going to be my life."

"Eddie, what you don't seem to be getting here is I'm not against you playing basketball. I'm all for it, but you need to concentrate on studies first. You graduate from high school with honors, go to a prestigious university and play basketball there if you make the team. You must look at other options as well. Be practical."

Eddie felt a tinge of *déjà vu*. He heard the same exact words from Byron Thompson this afternoon.

Mom added, "Your father is right. He was an exceptional football player during his college days, but he opted to go into business for himself. And look where we are now. I played some basketball myself, but we didn't have a professional league at that time. I knew that sports wasn't the answer, so I went into teaching."

"Pops, mom, you have all the answers, don't you?"

"Edward, don't take that tone with us," Dad warned. "You think about what we're saying and you'll realize that we're right."

"Father knows best," Eddie answered sarcastically.

"Eddie," Mom said, "we're not telling you to give up basketball."

"Then what are you saying?" Eddie sighed deeply. This was getting nowhere, and Eddie realized it. He remained silent for a while as he stared at his half-eaten salad.

"There will be no more talk about basketball tonight," Dad announced boldly. "You will start on your project tonight after dinner. There's no negotiating here."

Eddie looked at his dad disappointedly. "Well then, I wanna be excused now and go up to my room. I lost my appetite."

Dad frowned, rubbing his chin. "You will eat your dinner, and then you can go up to your room."

"Whatever." Eddie shook his head in disgust and mumbled under his breath. "What do you guys know anyway?"

"What's that?"

As Eddie grabbed his fork, he looked up and said, "Nothing, pops. Nothing at all."

There was a long awkward silence as the family resumed eating their dinner. Eddie was angry, but he knew that his parents meant business, so it was best not to say anything at all. But why couldn't they understand how he felt? Playing basketball was the ticket to success and riches. Any other job was just a job.

Feeling the awkwardness, Mom spoke, "Eddie, I know you have a game tomorrow, but can you pick Aaron up from school? I can't do it."

Eddie didn't want to obey, but he bit his tongue. "No problem, mom. I'll do it. But I got practice, so I may be a little late."

"No problem," Mom said sweetly. "I'll just inform his teacher that you'll be coming by a bit late."

"Sure," Eddie said with as much sincerity he could muster up. "I'll be there."

CHAPTER 6

The Spirits of Basketball Past

Eddie was walking with Alicia to class. He was still a bit upset about yesterday's events with his parents. But if there was something to be excited about, it was the call from Herbert Waters. If anything, Alicia would probably be thrilled about the phone call and encouraging about the whole situation. She, too, was a basketball player.

"So, this guy, Herbert Waters has been calling Eddie Holder for a whole week now," Eddie exaggerated boastfully. "And he just loves Eddie Holder. He thinks that Eddie Holder has the stuff to go pro right after high school."

Alicia said nothing.

"Girl, you should be happy for Eddie Holder," Eddie said. "Eddie Holder is gonna go places, and we gonna do it together. Eddie Holder is gonna make his best girl happy."

"I don't want to burst your bubble, but what happens if you don't make it?" Alicia asked innocently enough. "Shouldn't you have a back-up plan?"

"Not you, too?" Eddie opened his eyes wide. "You my girl, and you should be supporting me—Eddie Holder."

Alicia put her hand on Eddie's arm. "I do, Eddie, but I'm just worried about you. You don't seem to be thinking things through anymore. You're so different. You're not the Eddie Holder that I used to know."

"People change, and the Eddie Holder that you used to know was a chump. This is the real Eddie Holder."

Eddie thumped his chest with pride.

"The old Eddie Holder was kind and gentle. He was a smart, caring and cute guy…he was the one I fell in love with. I don't even know you anymore."

"Then maybe you should take off. Go hang out with that momma's boy, Richie Sykes. He's more your speed."

"Hey, that's not fair," Alicia said angrily. "I'm trying to support you, but you're not making it easy. You're not listening to what I have to say."

"Oh, I'm listening to you. Just like I'm listening to everybody else, but they all say the same thing, and they all wrong." Eddie shook his head. "Everybody's telling me that I don't have what it takes. The only person who's on my side is Herbert Waters."

"Eddie, it's not that. I'm just worried that all the things you have planned won't come true. You need to be realistic about your chances."

"Girl," Eddie sneered at Alicia. "I can't believe you don't have confidence in me."

"I do. It's just that…"

"Get out of my face, girl. Eddie Holder don't need someone who doesn't believe."

Eddie walked off angrily down the hallway, leaving Alicia behind.

"Oh, Eddie…"

Walking into his trigonometry class, Eddie was, once again, piping mad at the world. It wasn't right that no one was behind him anymore. And with Alicia now siding with everybody else, it not only made Eddie angry but it disappointed him even more. He would prove everybody wrong.

He slammed his trigonometry book down on his desk angrily and sat down in his chair and tried to calm down. But almost immediately, he realized that there was something different—something weird—about the class today and looked around. There was not a single soul in the classroom, not even the teacher, Mr. Higgins.

"Hey, where is everybody?" Eddie said to himself. "What's going on here?"

"Funny, you should ask," a voice said, which sounded distinctly familiar to Eddie.

Eddie turned to his left, where his teacher's desk was located, and saw Slamm Dunkk lying on his side atop the desk. Slamm Dunkk had a huge grin on his face.

"You, again?" Eddie's eyes widened in disbelief. "Why can't you just leave Eddie Holder alone?"

Ignoring Eddie's question, Slamm Dunkk shook his head sadly and said, "So you managed to turn another person against you. Tsk, tsk, tsk…Young Eddie, when are you ever going to learn?"

Eddie said nothing and just glared at Slamm Dunkk.

Slamm Dunkk jumped off the desk and walked over to Eddie. "You know something, Edward. I am sooo tired of your act. I would rather be reading a book by Ernest Hemingway or reading history books on Western Civilization or even playing hoops than helping your sorry butt out. But, then again, if I don't help you, who's going to? Herbert Waters?! That's a laugh."

"Don't be dissing Eddie Holder's main dawg. He's all the help that Eddie Holder needs." Eddie gestured at Slamm Dunkk in dismissal. "Eddie Holder don't need your help. He knows what he's doing."

"Pish-posh, Edward, I beg to differ, but like I said before, it's my job to show you the way…the right way whether you like it or not."

"Just get outta here!" Eddie demanded.

"I don't think so," Slamm Dunkk replied as he pointed a finger at Eddie.

From Slamm Dunkk's fingertips, a beam of twinkling lights shot out and began to envelop Eddie's body.

"Hey, what's going on?" Eddie tried to move but he couldn't.

The lights surrounded Eddie. And then, like magic, Eddie began to dissolve away, starting with his feet, then his legs, and then his upper torso.

"Helpppp….."

Poof! Eddie was gone from the face of the earth!

The kaleidoscope was a black vacuum with numerous florescent-colored geometric objects floating randomly and lazily about like stars dancing in space. At first glance, the kaleidoscope with its fresh air seemed like a place of natural simplistic beauty—but it was nothing of the sort. The kaleidoscope was actually a cold and lonely place, offering no happiness or warmth; it was truly a place of vast emptiness that went on for an eternity. There were no living beings around for light years, and it was in this sad and isolated kaleidoscope that Eddie Holder found himself materializing, all alone and scared.

His heart racing, Eddie Holder didn't know what to do or how to react to this mystifying location; it was certainly no basketball court. It wasn't even a tangible place that Eddie could put a name to. He had never experienced anything like this in his life, and it made Eddie feel like a prisoner forced into solitary confinement, despite the colorful shapes that floated past him.

All Eddie could do was stand quietly and watch the odd shapes float aimlessly by him. In their endless flight, the colorful objects were quite mesmerizing and seemingly harmless. And on a whim, Eddie reached over to grab a hold of one, but to his surprise, it zapped him with a jolting electrical charge and he howled in pain.

Bent over, Eddie blew on his hand trying to get the stinging to subside. He was so concerned about his hand, he was thoroughly unaware of the three different colored shapes—gold, green and red—shooting over in front of him. The size of hummingbirds, the shapes bobbed up and down excitedly, emitting a low buzzing sound. It was as though their intention was to catch Eddie's attention.

Eddie heard the buzzing sound, and for a brief second, he glanced up and took notice of the dancing objects. But thinking nothing of them, he went back to blowing on his hand. This did not sit well with the green colored shape. Its sound rising to a slightly higher pitch, it bobbed up and down highly agitated and rammed into Eddie's forehead. The image itself was as silly as some housefly trying to stop a rhinoceros in its track.

But the contact was far from miniscule. The impact threw Eddie back and he fell on his rump for the second time in as many days. This was getting a bit old, and with agitation taking over his other emotions for a split second, Eddie rose up to give the green shape a piece of his mind. But to Eddie's shock and horror, the three shapes had grown to monstrous proportions, and they were now in the process of transforming into hideous monsters. First heads, then muscular torsos, then arms and legs…

Eddie's imagination got the better of him; he envisioned himself being torn apart from limb to limb as the horrendous creatures fought over which body parts they wanted to devour. Eddie wanted to escape, but he couldn't move, paralyzed with too much fear. He let out a couple of blood-curdling screams, but it was really no use. Eddie was so far removed from human civilization the chance of someone coming to rescue him was probably zilch to none.

Covering his face, Eddie whined, "This isn't happening…this isn't happening to Eddie Holder…"

And then a voice said, "Hey, calm down, buddy!"

With his face still covered, Eddie spread his fingers out to see who had spoken, and he couldn't believe his eyes. Standing before him were not the three horrible creatures that he had imagined but three very tall human-like specters.

All donning capes with hoods on, the three specters were dressed in basketball warm-ups. Two were of African-American descent, one dressed in gold and the other dressed in red. The third was Caucasian and his sweats were emerald green.

The three spirits seemed vaguely familiar to Eddie, but it didn't seem likely. This place had to be playing tricks on Eddie's mind. There was no way that this was happening.

Eddie removed his hands and squeaked, "This can't be. You guys are…"

The Caucasian spirit held his hand up. "No, we're not whom you think we are."

"That's right," the African-American spirit, who was dressed in gold, said as he took off his hood and flashed Eddie a huge smile that could brighten even the heart of Osama Bin Laden. His big round eyes were alert yet warm, and the general feeling that he gave off was that he was a well-respected and charismatic leader.

He continued on, "We're the Spirits of Basketball Past. Slamm Dunkk asked us to help out. I'm Perseus, and this here is my good pal, Aquila."

Aquila acknowledged Eddie by taking off his hood and bowing his head slightly. With fair skin and blonde hair, Aquila could have been mistaken for any regular Joe on the street—a schoolteacher, a traveling salesman, or even a car mechanic—but there were qualities that separated Aquila from that regular Joe: His piercing blue eyes and his stern but focused expression—the "game face"—that seemed to be plastered on his face permanently. Eddie didn't know exactly what it was that intimidated him so, but he sensed the sheer force and strength of Aquila.

Perseus nodded his head toward the Spirit in red. "That's Pegasus."

Pegasus nodded his shaven head at Eddie coolly. "How do you do?"

With a pierced left ear, Pegasus had the body of a true athlete. He was quite handsome, and there was an unmistakable swagger yet graceful air about him. His manner seemed to combine flair and substance all at once. There was certainly something dynamic about his whole being.

Eddie knew that he was overmatched, but at the same time, he couldn't show his fear. He wasn't going to be bullied around by these so-called Spirits of Basketball Past, or whatever they called themselves.

Taking a deep breath, he put on a brave front. "Who are you retards, anyway? What's Eddie Holder doing here? Why are you doing this to him? Answer his questions."

"If you stopped yapping, you'll find out," Aquila interjected.

With a frown, Aquila stared directly into Eddie's eyes. His eyes were as relentless and alert as a hawk's. Unable to do a thing, Eddie could only look away.

Perseus said, "Let's not waste any more time here. Pegasus, whenever you're ready…"

"No time like the past," Pegasus said. "Of course, the pun is definitely intended."

Stretching his long muscular arms out, he clapped his hands, creating a thunderous sound. The kaleidoscope vibrated violently, and the odd peculiar shapes danced around and fused together, turning into larger familiar shapes like desks, a blackboard and so on. The whole environment had changed magically in front of Eddie's eyes, and the once barren black hole was now replaced by a classroom full of elementary school students in a matter of seconds.

"What's going on here?" Eddie looked over at Pegasus. Perseus and Aquila were now gone.

Pegasus pointed at the kids in the classroom. And without a protest, Eddie looked carefully at the kids in the room, noticing something oddly familiar about one of the students who stood in front of the classroom giving some sort of presentation.

"Hey!" Eddie exclaimed. "That's Eddie Holder when he was younger."

Eddie moved in closer and tried to get the attention of the younger Eddie. He stood in front of him and waved frantically, but the younger Eddie continued to give his presentation without pausing. It was as if the older Eddie didn't exist at all.

"Hel-lo…homie!" the older Eddie called. "Can you hear me?"

"They can't see you, Edward," Pegasus explained. "You're a phantom in this dimension. This is your past life."

Eddie rolled his eyes, went back to where Pegasus was and watched with his arms crossed, not amused.

"So this concludes my historical presentation on Jackie Robinson. I hope you enjoyed it," the younger Eddie said to the class.

"Baseball?" the older Eddie yelled. "Eddie Holder don't even like baseball no more."

Pegasus shot a stern look at Eddie. "But you did at one point, remember?"

Eddie gave a small groan. "Yeah, Eddie Holder remembers, and he sort of remembers this presentation, too. Eddie Holder must have been out of his mind to do something like this."

"You did your presentation on Jackie Robinson because it's an important aspect of your heritage and sports history. But, no, you can't worry about trivial stuff like that anymore because all Eddie Holder cares about is Eddie Holder," Pegasus scolded. "Now, will you kindly shut your mouth and continue to watch what's going on."

"Wait, Eddie Holder understands now. You guys are trying to convince Eddie Holder to play baseball." He pointed at Pegasus rudely. "You tried to play baseball once and failed, so now you want Eddie Holder to try so that you can live your dream through Eddie Holder."

Pegasus rolled his eyes. *Just exactly who did this kid think he was, shooting his mouth off like that?*

"In the first place, I don't know what you're blithering about. I'm not who you think I am, and I've never played baseball. And the second thing, if you don't stop referring to yourself as Eddie Holder and you don't stop talking in general, I'll see to it that you'll never talk again."

Eddie snorted. "Yeah, right!"

"I don't think you want to talk to me like that," Pegasus warned.

"Whatcha gonna do? Make Eddie Holder's mouth disappear?"

It seemed that Eddie Holder had gotten over his initial fear, and the more time they spent together, the more loud-mouthed and confident he became.

"I really don't want to do this, but it looks like I have no choice."

Pegasus produced a tiny basketball the size of a tennis ball out of nowhere and whipped it into Eddie's wide-open mouth as if it were a basketball hoop. The impact of the ball shooting into his mouth shocked Eddie, and his eyes began to water. He tried to pry the ball out of his mouth, but it wouldn't budge.

"Umph, gmph, whmph…"

With teary eyes, he looked at Pegasus in panic.

"Is Eddie Holder going to be quiet now?"

Eddie nodded his head vigorously like a bobble head doll.

"Good," Pegasus said, and with a flick of his hand, the basketball disappeared from Eddie's mouth.

Immediately, Eddie shouted out, "You didn't have to do that to Eddie Hol…"

Pegasus shot Eddie a stern look and wiggled a long slender finger. Eddie reacted by covering his mouth right away. He now knew that Pegasus meant serious business, and it would be best not to cause any more trouble. He would have to behave obediently every step of the way, if there was any chance of getting back to his reality in one piece.

Looking down, Eddie said sadly, "I'll be quiet now."

Pegasus nodded his head with understanding and pointed at the younger Eddie talking to his young and sweet looking teacher, Miss Lane.

Eddie chimed in excitedly, "Oh, yeah, I forgot about Miss Lane. She was beautiful and nice. She could get me to study any subject."

"Shhh!" Pegasus hushed, putting his index finger to his lips.

The younger Eddie asked, "Miss Lane…"

"Yes, Eddie." Miss Lane smiled.

"I know I finished my presentation…"

"Which was absolutely brilliant," Miss Lane interrupted.

"Thank you," Eddie said, "but while I was doing this presentation, I did an extra presentation. Do you think that I could show it to the class after all the other presentations are done?"

Miss Lane asked, "What is it about?"

"It's about George Washington Carver. It's one of the topics."

"Yes, it is," Miss Lane said. "It's wonderful that you want to do more, but, Eddie, you only had to do one presentation."

The younger Eddie blushed. "I know that, Miss Lane. It's not that I want extra credit or anything, but I just love to learn new things. History is just so much fun. I think we can learn a lot from history. If I had time, I would have done another presentation on Albert Einstein. Now, he's a genius."

As the present Eddie watched the interaction with Miss Lane, he was forced to remember that he was once a kid who was so enthusiastic about learning new things. But Eddie was fairly sure that he was no longer this Eddie Holder anymore. He was a different person now. He had another goal in life—basketball—and no one, not even this Spirit, Pegasus, or Slamm Dunkk, for that matter, was going to stop him from playing. Yet, with the past looming right before him, the nagging feeling that maybe basketball wasn't the definitive answer was slowly beginning to cross the back of his mind.

Pegasus looked over at Eddie. He wasn't a mind reader, but he knew that Eddie was beginning to second-guess his decisions and asked coolly, "Do you love basketball that much? Is it really a part of you?"

Eddie bit his lower lip. He was teetering…*Maybe it's not…maybe, I'm doing it all wrong…Hey, wait a minute…what's happening to me? What's wrong with me? Why am I having doubts? I do love basketball, and no one's going to change my mind…I think…*

"Yes, I do," Eddie said. But his tone of voice had sounded very meek and lacked passion.

"Do you now?" Pegasus said, looking at Eddie.

Eddie just nodded his head meekly, not wanting to say anymore that would further betray his confusion.

Knowing that he had gotten the better of Eddie, Pegasus just chuckled to himself and looked back to the younger Eddie Holder and Miss Lane.

Miss Lane said, "You know that you'll get an A on your Jackie Robinson project, and, if time allows, you can talk about Carver since you made the effort to do another presentation. I'll give you the extra credit."

"Thanks a bunch, Miss Lane."

"But tell me, Eddie," Miss Lane said. "Why are you working so hard?"

"Because I want to go to the best college and study history. Maybe I can help the world or something."

"That's really admirable, Eddie. I expect only great things from you."

Eddie blushed again. "Sure thing, Miss Lane. Well, I'll see you tomorrow."

With glee, Eddie rushed out of the room to meet his friends who were waiting out in the hallway.

"Do you remember that encounter?" Pegasus asked.

The older Eddie looked down and didn't say anything.

"Well?"

Eddie mumbled weakly, "Yeah...but, you know, the past is the past. What was important then is not important now. I'm going to play basketball..."

"Yeah, whatever, Edward," Pegasus said. "Come on, there's still a couple of more places that you have to visit. See you around, kid."

Pegasus snapped his fingers and disappeared instantly. Along with him, the classroom with Miss Lane looking fondly out the door at the younger Eddie vanished into thin air as well. Now, Eddie found himself once again in the lonely black vacuum with the funny shapes floating around him. Only this time he wasn't alone. Aquila was right next to Eddie.

"Oh, it's you..." Eddie said timidly. He wasn't sure what was in store for him next, and it made him very uncomfortable.

From under his cape, Aquila pulled out a basketball and began twirling it with his right index finger. "We still have a lot of ground to cover."

Aquila tossed the basketball up into the empty space, and the basketball rose high above both of them. Then it stopped abruptly, frozen in the black space above.

Concentrating on the still ball, Aquila began waving his arms like a conductor of an orchestra, and the ball began to spin and dance, leaving a trail of gold pixie dust. Like mist from a waterfall, the gold pixie dust drifted down around both Eddie and Aquila, transforming what once was a black vacuum into a three-dimensional oil painting.

In awe, Eddie spun around looking at the surrounding environment and recognized it almost at once. It was the basketball courts of El Camino Park, where Eddie often played basketball with his friends as a middle school student in the past and even now as a high school student.

Around Eddie, students suddenly began popping up out of nowhere frozen in place, playing basketball happily. Eddie recognized some of the students, and he couldn't help but feel the all-around warmth and joy as he studied the cheerful expressions of the kids in their various poses. It was as though he were inside a Norman Rockwell painting.

"Awesome," Eddie whispered.

Aquila asked, "What's that?"

Eddie covered his mouth automatically. He could feel that he was losing himself again…growing even more uncertain of the path he had chosen to take. *No! This must stop right here and now! I will not give in to their powers!*

"Nothing," Eddie lied, trying to be tough. "I said nothing at all."

"Whatever you say," Aquila said as the ball flew back into his hands.

Aquila gazed at the frozen painting around them, admiring his masterful artwork. He then glanced at Eddie, who was looking down at the ground.

"You recognize this place, don't you?"

Eddie barely nodded his head.

"Good, then let it begin." Aquila snapped his fingers and the students around them came to life all of sudden and began to run up and down the basketball court.

"Just remember, don't try anything. They can't see you, you know," he reminded Eddie.

Eddie finally looked up at Aquila and muttered, "What do you think I am? Stupid or something?"

"I don't think you want me to answer that question," Aquila shot back, pointing toward one of the kids shooting a basketball all alone at the far end of the basketball courts. Eddie was expecting to see a younger version of himself, but he was shocked to see that the kid was Richie Sykes.

Then, instinctively, Eddie knew what was going to happen next. And he didn't like it one bit. He closed his eyes, covered his ears with both of his hands and shook his head frantically, hoping that it would all go away.

Aquila commented, "Be a man and face the music, Edward."

Eddie stopped shaking his head and just stared at the ground for a minute. This was sheer torture for him, but as much as he disliked what was happening, he realized that there was no way around it. What was about to happen would forever remain a part of him no matter what he tried to do. With a deep sigh, Eddie looked up finally and watched the past unfold.

While Richie Sykes continued to play basketball by himself, a younger Eddie Holder ran to him.

"Hey, you just moved in next to us a couple of days ago, huh?" Eddie said enthusiastically.

Richie retrieved the ball and smiled at Eddie. "Yeah."

"We're short a guy. You wanna play with us?"

"Thanks, but no thanks." Richie looked at the ball that he was cradling. "I'm not that good, and you guys are a lot taller than I am."

Eddie came over to Richie and put his arm around his shoulders in a friendly manner. "Don't be shy. We're just here to have fun. Besides, if I don't welcome you to my neighborhood, what kind of guy would I be? C'mon."

"I don't know," Richie said softly.

"It'll be fun," Eddie said cheerfully. "My name is Eddie."

"I'm Richie Sykes. Okay, I'll play, but I don't want anybody making fun of me or anything like that."

Eddie dragged Richie over to the where the other kids were playing basketball, and they began to play. Richie was on Eddie's team, and the two made quite a pair. Of course, they weren't exactly the famed dynamic duo of Karl Malone and John Stockton, but they were in sync with each other, which was pretty remarkable considering they were only middle school students and had never played together as a team before.

Regardless of the fact that Richie was younger and smaller than the other kids, Richie tried his hardest. He jumped high to grab rebounds off missed shots and ran down the court as fast as he could to get back on defense. Eddie saw how hard he was trying and looked to pass him the ball as much as possible, and each time Richie caught a pass from Eddie, he was usually open under the basket and made lay-ups easily.

This went on throughout the course of the game, and Eddie's team easily won game after game. When dusk came around and it grew dark, everybody called it quits, gave each other hi-fives and went home excitedly. Eddie and Richie walked back home together.

The present Eddie Holder and Aquila followed the two middle-school students. Aquila was half expecting Eddie to shoot off at the mouth, but surprisingly enough, Eddie hadn't uttered a single word. Perhaps he was getting the picture after all.

"I thought you said you weren't that good," the young Eddie Holder said.

Richie tried to hold back a big smile but couldn't. "I'm not. I just do the best that I can. That's all."

"Well, I'm glad you decided to play," Eddie said, slapping Richie on the shoulders. "It was really fun playing with you."

Richie laughed. "I had fun, too. Too bad we couldn't play longer."

"Well, I couldn't anyway. I have a major science project that I want to finish by tonight. I really shouldn't have been playing basketball."

The two of them continued to walk home, and when they reached Eddie's house, Eddie said, "Hey, if I finish my science project tonight, you wanna play some hoops tomorrow?"

"I don't know if I can. I have to do some chores around the house first," Richie replied. "And then I have to work on this comic book for my art project."

Eddie became excited. "Wow, you're drawing a comic book? That's cool, dude."

A bit embarrassed, Richie shuffled his feet a little. "Yeah, I like to draw and I like to write, too. One of these days, I want to write the greatest American novel."

"Well, I'll be the first one to read it." Eddie laughed aloud. "Don't forget me when you're famous!"

"Hey, that's my line!" Richie pointed a finger at Eddie. "Don't forget about me when you're a big basketball star."

Eddie made a funny face. "Rich, you're kidding, right? I love to play basketball, but I don't plan on becoming pro."

"Famous last words, huh?" Aquila whispered into the present Eddie's ears.

Eddie ignored Aquila's biting words as he continued to watch and relive his past.

"But, you're so awesome!" Richie was shocked.

"Hey, you may think I'm awesome, but there's plenty better than me. Maybe this is corny, but I plan to use my brains for my career."

Eddie thumped his chest proudly.

Richie shrugged. "I guess you're right."

"I know I am," Eddie said. "Hey, instead of playing basketball, can I check out your artwork? I betcha it's really cool stuff."

"Okay." Richie shuffled his feet embarrassedly.

"Cool, Richie." Eddie was excited. "Why don't you come on over here like around 1 or something tomorrow."

Richie nodded his head. "See ya then, buddy."

Richie and Eddie gave each other hi-fives, and then Richie ran home excitedly. Eddie looked on, feeling good that he had made a new friend, who seemed to have a lot in common with him.

"Well?" Aquila asked.

Eddie remained silent, and Aquila gathered that Eddie Holder was at odds with his own past and his current feelings.

"There's still some more to see," Aquila said. "So long."

Aquila clapped his hands lightly and disappeared into thin air. In his place, Perseus appeared out of nowhere. Eddie didn't seem to notice any of this. He was too deep in thought.

"Let's go, Eddie." Perseus tapped Eddie on the shoulder.

Startled, Eddie turned to look at Perseus. "Oh, it's you."

"We have to go now."

"Yeah, sure," Eddie said with a resigned tone. He was drained mentally and wanted to go back home to the real world.

"Well, here we go," Perseus said as he produced a magic wand from his sleeve and waved it at Eddie with a flourish.

But nothing happened!

A bit surprised, Eddie checked himself out to see if everything was intact and let out a big sigh of relief once he realized everything was a-okay. And then he gave Perseus a smug look as if to say he messed up. But at that exact moment, Perseus began to grow in size rapidly.

Eddie screamed out, "Oh, lordy!"

Eddie's voice came out as a high-pitched unnatural squeak, and then it dawned on him that it wasn't Perseus who was growing, but it was he himself who was actually shrinking in size.

Growing smaller and smaller, Eddie gave a frantic look at the colossal Perseus. Good-naturedly, Perseus just smiled back at Eddie and waved good-bye with his wand.

Like a little mouse, Eddie squealed, "What's going onnnn…"

"…hheerre?!"

And just like that, Eddie felt normal again. But to make absolutely sure, he checked his arms and legs; cracked his knuckles; bent his knees a few times; patted his body down; and tested his voice out. Everything seemed to be back intact.

With a bit of relief, Eddie stretched his body and casually looked around at his surroundings. He was at home in his own bedroom. But it wasn't his bedroom of the present. The decoration of his room was plain and simple with a few posters of his favorite athletes and movie stars. It wasn't overkill like the way his current room was with all the basketball memorabilia.

"Wondering why you're here?" Perseus's voice boomed as he appeared out of nowhere.

"Yeah, what's going on?" Eddie asked.

Perseus answered, "Well, watch and see."

And, as if on cue, the door opened with Eddie and Richie entering the bedroom. Quite upset, Richie threw down his books on Eddie's bed and sat in one corner on the floor. He bent his knees, bringing them close to his chest. He covered his face with his hands and began to sob.

Eddie plopped down on the bed, looking up at the ceiling. He could hear Richie's sobs getting louder. He felt sorry for him, but feeling sympathy for his friend wasn't going to help him out. Eddie figured he needed some tough love.

"Geez, Richie," Eddie said as he continued to stare up at the ceiling. "It's not the end of the world."

Between the sobs, Richie said, "This has got to be the worst day of my life."

"Don't worry, you'll have worse ones than this!" Eddie sat up on the bed. "Missing a shot and losing the game is not the worst thing that can happen."

Richie looked at Eddie angrily. "Yeah? Then what's worse?"

"Not playing at all," Eddie answered quietly.

"Oh…"

Shaking his head, Eddie said, "I'm just a sophomore, but I made the varsity team. I hardly get to play games, but I still work hard at my game because I figure I'll get my chance. Maybe not this year, but at least, I still have two more years of high school. So don't give me any of this crybaby stuff about how you lost the game. At least, you're playing."

"But it's only the freshman team," Richie said.

"I don't care if it's underwater basketball weaving!" Eddie's voice rose in pitch. "You're playing! You made the team easily. You're the captain of the team, and everybody likes you. What more do you want?"

"I wanted to play on varsity this year," Richie declared.

"So this is where it's coming from?" Eddie shook his head again. "Gimme a break, man. So what if you didn't make the team this year? Coach knows you got skills, and I always talk you up. You'll definitely make it next year. I got faith in you. I think you're better than a lot of the other guys."

Eddie paused for a second. "In fact, I think you're better than me."

"Really?" Richie's eyes lightened up.

"Yeah," Eddie said emphatically. "You're just a freshman, and life's always tough the first year. What are you trying to prove anyway? You're not Superman!"

The older Eddie Holder looked on and sighed. He remembered this day well, yet he had tucked it away deep down in his memory banks. This was the first time he had ever confessed that Richie was a better player, but it was also the last time. Since his days of arriving as an all-star prep, Eddie stopped admitting that Richie had more skills. And just because he was forced to recall his past, he wasn't about to start up again now. *Never...not in a million years!*

Richie thought it over for a minute. Then he said, "I guess I'm acting like a big baby."

"You are a big baby!" Eddie smiled. "Big baby freshman."

"Hey!"

"I know you'll make it next year, so don't worry. But I tell you what. If you don't make varsity next year like I said..." past Eddie said.

Then present Eddie mouthed the words along with past Eddie, "...then I'll quit the team, and we can go do something else."

"No way!" Richie exclaimed.

The younger Eddie smiled. "That's right, no way. Because you'll make the team and we'll be El Camino's 1-2 punch next year. C'mon, let's go get some ice cream now because I have a lot of studying to do tonight."

The two left the room, and the present Eddie stared into space in a daze. He sank down to his knees and let his head hang down low.

"Why is this happening to me now?" Eddie muttered. He could feel himself losing his grip on things by the second. Everything had been determined in his mind. He would become a professional basketball star with the help of Shark Waters, and nothing would stand in his way. Yet, after witnessing his past, Eddie's emotions was all jumbled up, his heart was churned inside and out, and he was discouraged.

Suddenly, Eddie stood up and glared at Perseus. "Dis is whack! I don't need none of this. I worked too hard to get where I'm at, and you're not gonna mess it up for me. No one is! Not you, not that freakin' Slamm Dunkk, not Pegasus, and not even Aquila. No one, you hear me!"

Perseus just shook his head sadly. "Why does it always have to be about Eddie Holder all the time?"

Eddie turned away, having no answer.

"Well?"

"Just leave me alone…" Eddie's voice was feeble. "I've had enough of you guys."

"Well, if that's the way you feel," Perseus said, pulling out his magic wand again.

"Hey!" Eddie screamed. "Not again…"

Perseus waved the wand, and Eddie shrank again. In less than a second, Eddie was gone, and what remained of his entire body was just a tiny puddle of sweat.

Blowing the tip of his smoking wand, Perseus muttered softly, "Now you see him, now you don't."

Eddie shot up from his seat and shouted out, "Yeow, what's going on here?"

There was laughter around Eddie, and he realized that his trigonometry classmates were sitting around him, snickering at him. He was back in his world, and he felt a sense of relief although it was a bit embarrassing at the moment.

"Well, I'm glad that you decided to wake up from your nap," Eddie's trigonometry teacher said in a slightly agitated voice.

"My bad. I was in another world," Eddie responded.

His words sounded strange as they left his mouth, and he wondered immediately how much stranger they sounded to his teacher.

The trig teacher raised an eyebrow. "Oh, you were, were you? Would you like to tell that to the dean?"

"Yes…I mean, no…" Eddie was a bit thrown off balance. He didn't know what to say. "It won't happen again, Mr. Higgins, I promise."

There was neither a response nor any movement from Mr. Higgins. His eyes were glossed over as he stared back without blinking, as if he were some sort of a mannequin. In fact, the entire class had stopped moving as well, frozen in time.

"Uh, Mr. Higgins…"

"He can't hear you," a familiar voice said, and out from behind Mr. Higgins, who was an extremely large man, Slamm Dunkk appeared.

Eddie sighed, "I shoulda known."

"Well, how was your trip, old boy?" Slamm Dunkk had on a mischievous smile.

Just the sight of Slamm Dunkk wound up Eddie. And no matter how confused he was now, he wasn't going show it to Slamm Dunkk. He wouldn't give him the slightest satisfaction.

"You ain't going to win, Slamm." Eddie stood up fearlessly. "Whatever you do to me, I ain't changin' my mind."

Slamm Dunkk shrugged as if he didn't care. "This isn't a contest."

"I'm gonna play basketball! Ain't nobody gonna stop me!" Eddie announced, thumping his chest with his large fists.

"Well, at least, we rid you of that disgusting habit of referring to yourself as Eddie Holder. But we really have to do something about that atrocious grammar of yours." Slamm Dunkk gave the biggest smile he could give to Eddie. "Hey, you may act tough, Mr. Holder, but I know exactly what you're going through. You can't fool me. I'm not finished with you yet, Edwardo!"

Eddie clenched his teeth. "Bring it on. I'll bring you down, pal."

"I'm looking forward to it. See you around, kiddo." Slamm Dunkk saluted Eddie and then snapped his fingers, disappearing as quickly as he had appeared in the trigonometry class.

"You'll see," Eddie whispered to himself. "I will play basketball…"

CHAPTER 7

I'll Do It My Way

Eddie was in "the zone." He had taken ten shots from long range without a miss, and some of his teammates just stood by amazed at what they were witnessing. Eddie's eleventh shot was way beyond the 3-point line. Nothing but net. He then dribbled the ball closer to the basket and threw up another shot, this time 20 feet away. The ball swished in barely disturbing the net.

Eddie was beginning to feel whole again. Each time he touched the ball and made a basket, he felt alive. And the fact that he had arranged to meet with Herbert Waters right after practice instead of after the game helped ease the pain of the nightmare with the Spirits of Basketball Past and Slamm Dunkk. It was good to know that at least one person was behind him 110 percent of the way.

After the unpleasant episode with the Spirits, Eddie felt a bit sick physically and mentally, and he didn't know whom he could lean on for help. If he told anybody—his teammates, Alicia, or his parents—about the Spirits, they would have all thought that he flipped his lid for sure. Thinking as calmly as he could, he decided to call Herbert Waters, and after talking to him during lunch on a pay phone, Eddie felt a little better. Shark Waters had comforted him with soothing words and had convinced him that he was making the right choice to play basketball professionally, and so, it was decided to meet after practice to discuss their future plans together. With Herbert Waters as his number one supporter, Eddie realized he had to shake away whatever doubts he had and move forward.

Eddie took another shot, this time from the free throw line, but it didn't even hit the rim. Air ball.

"My momma coulda made that shot," a voice said from behind.

Thinking that it might be Slamm Dunkk, Eddie turned around and yelled, "Just leave me alone, you jerk!"

He was immediately embarrassed to see that it was only Flash, who had made the joke. Flash was with Sam and Richie, and they walked over to Eddie.

"What? You can't even take a joke anymore, dawg." Flash said.

Eddie said, "My bad. I thought you were someone else."

Staring at Eddie oddly, Flash shrugged and then ran over to get a basketball from a rack. He drove to the basket and threw the ball forcefully against the backboard. The ball made its decline, and Flash caught it before it bounced, spun it up toward the basket with a lot of English, and laid it up and into the basket. Then, with his chest sticking out proudly, he strolled back over to Eddie and looked at him coolly. He was about to challenge Eddie to a game of horse but noticed how fatigued and pale looking Eddie was.

"Are you okay, man?" Flash asked with concern. "You look like you've seen a ghost or something. You don't look so hot."

"I'm cool. I just got a lot of things on mind," Eddie said.

"Like what? How many points you plan to score tonight?" Flash joked. "Or is it something else? Like how many times you don't plan on passing the ball?"

"That's enough, Flash," Sam warned.

"Gomen'nasai." Flash shrugged his shoulders. "Sor-ree…"

"Yeah," Richie said with concern. "Eddie, maybe you shouldn't play tonight."

Eddie shot a mean look at Richie. "What, taking my place as a starter is not good enough for you. Now, you don't want me to play? Oh, I'm starting tonight, and you're going back to the bench for good."

"C'mon, you know that's not what I meant, Eddie," Richie said.

"I don't care what you meant," Eddie said. "In fact, I don't care what you all think. All of you are just in my way to glory."

"Whatcha talking about?" Flash said. "Dawg, it's you who's messing this team up. Always hog-cheesing the ball and always trying to take credit for the win."

Sam added, "Although we're losing right now, at least we play as a team. And with Richie around, we don't have to worry about the finger pointing. We win as a team and we lose as a team."

"Forget about the team. It's time for individual glory." Eddie paused for a minute. "What's with all this team work and team effort bull? It's only high school basketball. I'm gonna go to the pros early, while you dawgs just waste your time here. In fact, I got me an agent who says that I can go pro right after high school. He says that I got loads of talent."

"Stop pulling our rickshaw," Flash said. "You lie like a dog."

"Ain't no lie," Eddie answered back. "It's all true."

Flash rolled his eyes, while Sam and Richie looked away. The guys weren't buying it.

"Sheez, I can't believe you guys don't believe me. You guys jealous or something?" Eddie shook his head in disgust. "Man, I don't even know why I waste my time with you losers!"

Angrily, Flash grabbed a basketball from the ground and flung it hard at Eddie. Eddie dropped the ball, shouting out in pain.

"*Baka nanjanai no ka!*" Flash snickered. "Boy can't even catch a pass. If your agent saw that, he'd drop you like a butt ugly chick. Dude, you need to stop dreaming. You ain't no LeBron James, and you ain't ever gonna be. You ain't even Richie Sykes."

"So you're saying that I don't got it?" Eddie came an inch away from Flash. "Well, I'll show you."

"Make your move," Flash yelled as he pushed Eddie away.

Eddie staggered back, but he managed to gain his balance and rush toward Flash. But Sam held Eddie back before anything could happen.

"Chill, dude," Sam said. "What's the matter with you?"

"Nothing. Just leave me alone," Eddie hollered as he pulled away from Sam's hold. "You guys just make me sick."

"What's going on here?" a voice boomed. It was the coach.

Sam scratched his head. "Nothing, coach. We're just getting psyched-up for tonight's game. That's all."

The coach said, "I would say, 'save it for tonight' but the game's been cancelled. There's structural damage to the other school's bleachers. Now, go run a mile, and then we'll have a scrimmage."

Groaning loudly, the team all rushed out to the track. As they left the gymnasium, Eddie glared at Flash angrily but did not retaliate. In his mind, he would show him up during scrimmage. In fact, he would show all of them up.

The coach and Byron Thompson watched from the bleachers as the team scrimmaged. There was definitely some edginess among the players, but they let it go, trusting it was a good motivator for competitiveness.

Flash dribbled the ball down the court and went to the corner. As Richie came to guard him, Flash whipped the ball to Eddie, who was open near the top of the key. Catching the ball, Eddie then bounced it as he surveyed the floor. He saw Sam get free in the low-post and cut through the lane, but rather than pass the ball to the open Sam, Eddie drove the lane.

When he penetrated the lane swiftly, Eddie recognized that he now had another option. From the corner of his eyes, he saw Flash wide open for a jumper when Richie came to help defend against his drive, but the better and simple option was still lofting the ball up to Sam so he could slam it home. However, Eddie chose none of them. Instead Eddie split two defenders—one being Richie—and spun around Sam's defender. And with his back to the basket, he threw the ball up and over his head, trying a circus shot. The ball bounced, not once, not twice, but three times on the rim before it finally nestled into the hole.

After the made basket, Eddie looked at Sam triumphantly while shooting him with a finger. Then, brazenly, he blew on the same finger, pretending it was the barrel of a six-shooter.

Sam came toward Eddie. "I was wide open. Why didn't you pass me the ball?"

Eddie picked up the ball and threw it at Sam sharply. Dodging the ball, Sam grabbed the front of Eddie's jersey and pulled him closer.

"Okay, okay, girls," the coach said running from the bleachers. "Break it up."

Byron pulled Sam away from Eddie.

"Holder, what's with that?" the coach asked. "You see an open man near the basket, and you pass it to him. It's that simple."

Eddie shrugged. "Sorry, coach. I didn't see him. Won't happen again."

"Fine, don't let it," the coach scolded Eddie. "Now, let's continue on with the scrimmage."

A player on the other team retrieved the ball and play resumed. Now, on defense, Eddie got in his defensive stance. He eyed his opponent quite alertly, and, when his opponent got ready to make a pass, Eddie stole the ball and ran down the court. It was a clear fast break, and just ahead of Eddie was Flash, who had a free path to the basket. It would be an easy two points, but Eddie chose to ignore his teammate. Eddie turned on his jets, twirled around one defender and ran directly to the basket, finger-rolling the ball into the basket with a fluid, silky motion.

"What was that, fool?" Flash asked.

"I couldn't make the pass," Eddie explained.

"That's a bunch of bull, and you know it." Flash shook his head in disgust. "What's with you, dawg?"

The coach came over to the players once again. "Eddie, I want to have a word with you."

Eddie pleaded, "Coach, I couldn't make the pass. There was a defender in my way."

"Holder, in my office. Now!" The coach pointed in the direction of the locker room.

Visibly upset, Eddie headed toward the locker room, and as he walked by Flash, Flash whispered, "Punk, you ain't got a clue."

Eddie turned around ready to fight Flash, but the coach grabbed him.

"Holder, I want you to cool it," the coach demanded. "I don't need you trying to steal the limelight all the time. You continue to act up this way, I may have no choice but to kick you off the team."

"Whatcha talking about, coach? You need me!"

Eddie quickly looked at Byron, who stood next to the coach, and Byron just frowned at him.

"What?" Eddie said angrily. "You don't think I'm right? I told you all. I couldn't make that pass. I ain't showboating."

Byron put his hand on Eddie's shoulder. "It's not just about the pass. It's your whole attitude, Eddie. If you can't trust your teammates, you're not part of the team."

Eddie threw up his hands. "Man, I don't believe any of this. I'm going home."

"Why don't you do that?" the coach said angrily. "And while you're at it, maybe you should think about why I shouldn't kick you off the team."

Eddie shot a dirty look at both the coach and Byron. He then looked behind him at his teammates, who were all standing in silence watching the entire incident.

"Can't stand being with you losers, anyway," Eddie mumbled under his breath and stomped off in a huff. "I don't need none of this. I don't need none of you."

Byron watched Eddie leave the gym, shaking his head sadly. "Coach, what are you going to do?"

"I don't think I have a choice, Byron," the coach answered. "Eddie Holder is off the team!"

It had turned out to be a rotten day for Eddie after all. Not only did the Spirits do a number on him, but he was also kicked out of practice for no good reason. Eddie couldn't help but feel that everyone had it in for him. Even Byron Thompson. But when Eddie thought about it, he really didn't like the self-righteous guy too much in the first place.

Now, it looked like the day was about to get worse for Eddie. Eddie had been sitting on the patio of the seaside restaurant, waiting for Herbert Waters for over a half hour. Already on his third refill of lemonade, he was tired of throwing breadcrumbs at the herons that were just waiting to get fed. Tired of all that was happening to him. Tired of all this waiting. He had to talk to Waters and make sure that he wasn't making the wrong choice. If anything, Waters would be the one to straighten him out. He would encourage him and give him strength. But he wasn't here. Had Waters forgotten about poor old Eddie?

Eddie took an anxious sip from his drink. Then another one.

Suddenly, it dawned on Eddie. Maybe this was another one of Slamm Dunkk's tricks. Maybe he was preventing Herbert Waters from meeting him. And if that was the case, Eddie thought a phone call to Waters was in order just to check and see.

As Eddie got off his seat to make the phone call, Herbert Waters came rushing onto the patio while talking on his cellular phone. Waters shook Eddie's hand and took a seat opposite from him.

Well, at least he showed up. Eddie sat back in his seat and relaxed a little.

"Okay, dude," Waters said on the phone. "I think we should hold out for more. We'll be okay. I'll be in touch."

Waters flipped the phone away and turned to give Eddie his undivided attention.

"I'm so sorry I'm late, my man." Shark smiled warmly at Eddie. "Duty calls. You know, no rest for the weary. So, what's up? You seemed upset when you called me this afternoon."

Eddie was uncertain about how to begin. He was quiet for a brief moment, thinking about what to say.

"Hey, Eddie, you can talk to me. I'm your buddy." Shark's words seemed very soothing.

"There are people who are against this." Eddie's voice came out weak. "And I don't know what to do."

"Hold onto your thought for a minute." Waters waved over a waitress and ordered some coffee and a chicken sandwich with onion rings on the side.

"Sorry, Eddie," Waters said. "I haven't eaten all day today. It's been that kind of day."

"Yeah, me, too."

"So, what people are you talking about, Eddie?" Shark knew very well that it was all Slamm Dunkk's doing that Eddie was in this funk. Somehow, he would have to put a stop to all of this, but, for now, he needed to reach Eddie by showing as much sincerity and warmth that he could. He had to show that he was on Eddie's side all the way.

"They, everybody. Nobody wants me to play basketball," Eddie announced.

In an exaggerated fashion, Shark stretched his arms out and exclaimed, "Is that all?"

"What do you mean is that all?" Eddie was disappointed with Waters' reaction.

Shark made an odd sound that may have been a laugh. "What are you worried about? My dear old friend, you need to relax. I got your back all the way."

The waitress came by and put his food and coffee on the table. Right away, Waters drank his coffee.

"Ah, nothing like bad coffee to end the day," Shark commented as he smiled at Eddie who looked as though he had been dragged by an eighteen-wheeler.

"You still have your reservations, don't you?" It was more of a statement than a question.

Eddie nodded his head slowly.

"You know about Michael Jordan getting cut from the varsity team when he was a sophomore, right?"

Again, another nod.

Shark gestured his arms in a dramatic fashion. "Obviously, there were forces against Michael playing basketball, but did he give up? No way! He used it as motivation to only get better, and we all know what happened to Michael."

"So don't let the people around you discourage you." Herbert took a long drink from his coffee. "You have what it takes to make the pros now. Believe me, I know, and to prove that I know what I'm talking about, this is what we're going to do."

Eddie still had his doubts, but he listened carefully to what his only support system had to say.

"You're a junior, right?"

Eddie answered, "Yes, I am."

"When are you going to turn seventeen?"

"In June."

"Perfect!" Shark clapped his hands loudly. "After the school year, we fly off to Europe and play some hoops there. You know, hone your skills."

"Europe?"

"Sure, I'm sure you already know this, but there are plenty of good European players who play professionally here. Nowitzki, Stojakovic, Divac, Gasol. And I'm sure there'll be more in the future."

"But what about finishing school?" Eddie felt weird asking the question. "What am I supposed to do?"

Shark waved his hands in a "not-to-worry" gesture. "No problem. They have programs over there. They have mentoring programs, so you never have to worry about being left alone. Their programs are truly superb. They not only train you on the court, but being that you're so young, they'll watch you off the court as well. It's really a great program. But the best part is that you don't have to be eighteen to play. Remember Tony Parker started pro ball at seventeen."

"Really? I can play professionally in Europe?" Eddie could feel himself getting excited all over again, and the more Herbert Waters spoke, the less dreadful the day's events became.

Shark had the kid hooked and poured it on. "That's right, and I can set you up. You play in Europe for two years, and then make a name for yourself over there. There are American scouts all over Europe looking for the next European Michael Jordan. And you can be it."

"What about my parents?"

Shark shrugged his shoulders. "What about your parents? They don't have to do anything. All they have to do is give parental consent, and that's it. But, then again, I do have to warn you."

Eddie asked, "About what?"

"Well, this is something that I don't like to talk about. It has to do with money."

Shark looked down, faking embarrassment. "There's an upfront fee to enter this mentoring program."

"Oh." Eddie was a bit disappointed. There was no way that his parents would pay that fee, let alone, give their blessings to Eddie to play basketball in Europe, of all places.

"It's not that bad," Shark said cheerfully. "The full fee is $25,000, half of it upfront and the other half of it when you leave for Europe. Of course, that doesn't include airfares."

"I don't think my parents will let me go."

Shark gave Eddie a big grin. "Don't worry about your parents. I can convince them in a heartbeat."

"But you don't know them. They want me to get a proper education. They're already bugging me about college."

"College, smollege…that's what's so great about the mentoring program," Shark continued to lie. "Although it's basically a mentoring program for basketball, you not only get an equivalent of a high school diploma, but you can continue on with extension classes for a college degree, if you choose."

"Oh, yeah?" Eddie could feel his heart dance with excitement. Maybe this mentoring program would convince his parents. Waters certainly had him convinced.

"Eddie, you're a bright and talented kid." Shark winked at Eddie. "Look at it this way. You can't lose. You're in Europe playing basketball professionally, which will automatically wash away your $25,000 fees. And at the same time, you're studying to get an equivalent of a high school diploma. How can your parents so no to that, huh?"

Eddie pondered it for a moment, looked at Shark and then said determinedly, "Okay, Herbert, I'll do it. But every time I start talking about b-ball, they don't listen, so you got to talk to them about it. And the sooner the better. If you talk to them, they'll listen."

Shark reached over and put his fat hands on Eddie's shoulder. Shark's grip was strong, and Eddie felt a momentary energy surge radiating from him. Eddie looked directly into Shark's face, and for a brief second, Eddie could have sworn Shark's eyes had flashed red with his face becoming a bit fleshier. But then he immediately dismissed it, realizing he was more fatigued than he realized.

Shark smiled warmly. "Good man. We can talk about my fees—which are totally reasonable, by the way—at a later date. But in the meantime, I'll talk to your parents. Perhaps tomorrow morning. I'll give them a call tonight and set something up. Heck, I could even have a contract drawn up when I meet them."

"Sweet!" Eddie clapped his hands. "Thanks a bunch, Herbert."

"No problem, Eddie." Shark gave Eddie another warm smile. "Oh, yeah, and one more thing."

"Yeah?"

"I'm your man, right? And I'm going to take care of you, right?"

Eddie nodded his head emphatically.

"Well, my dear boy, I realize that you've had an extremely hard day," Shark said with a twinkle in his eye. "And since it is my job to take care of you, I want you to be happy. I have a special gift just for you."

Reaching into his pants pocket, Shark held up a set of car keys and jingled it in front of Eddie's face. He was confident that this would be the *coup de grâce*. There was absolutely no way that Eddie would refuse the gift, and once he took the car keys, this would be just the beginning of Shark's victory over Slamm Dunkk. Just with his empty promises, he knew that he had won over Eddie's heart, and now, it was just a matter of bestowing gifts upon gifts and slowly stealing Eddie's soul.

Eddie looked bashfully at the car keys. "You're lending me your car?"

"Abso-friggin'-lutely!" Shark winked at Eddie. "And maybe if you take good care of it for the day, I'll let you use it for the whole week."

"No way!"

"You're my boy." Shark thought about P.T. Barnum, and he couldn't keep the evil smile across his face from spreading. "Forever…"

Shark's car was a sleek, black Nissan 350Z. The sun glinted strongly off the hood of the polished car in the parking lot. It was absolutely beautiful, and Eddie couldn't believe that Waters was entrusting him with it.

"Dat's so phat, Herbert," Eddie's eyes were just about bulging out. "Man, oh, man, I can't believe this is your car."

"It certainly is, but just think. Once you go pro, you can own 10 of these cars easily." Shark spread out his arms. "The world is your oyster."

Eddie put a hand on the hood and moved it back and forth. The car felt so smooth.

"I can really drive it all day?" Eddie was so excited about the prospect of driving the automobile, the nightmare he had experienced with the Spirits and the basketball team seemed all but a distant memory.

"That's what I said," Shark Waters said. "What, you just going to stare at it all day long? Try it on."

Thoroughly excited, Eddie hopped into the car and checked out the interior. It had leather upholstery that felt smooth to the touch, a cool navigational system, a sunroof, an impressive 6-CD changer, and a top-of-the-line mobile phone between the two seats.

"All this baby needs is heat-seeking missiles!" Shark remarked, as he leaned into the car. "You got any plans for tomorrow night?"

"Nah, wud up tomorrow night?"

Shark rubbed his chin slowly. "The way I figure it, by this time, tomorrow, all the paperwork will be done, and I'd say we could have a contract signing party in your honor. You know, an Eddie Holder coming out party. I'll make all the arrangements, invite a few of my celebrity friends, and you can invite whomever you want."

"Dat's so cool!"

"Good, I'll give you the details when I see you tomorrow morning," Shark said. "And I have one other gift for you."

Standing up straight, Shark took out his wallet from his back pocket and pulled out ten crisp one hundred dollar bills. He gave the bills to Eddie. Eddie gawked at the money in his hands, not knowing what to do.

"I'm not sure if I should," Eddie mumbled. "It don't seem right."

"Eddie Holder, I am going to take care of you. Consider this just a token of my appreciation for allowing me to be your agent."

"I don't know…"

"Just take the money and the car, and have a good time on me, okay?" Shark gave Eddie a wink. "Don't argument with me."

Eddie thought about this for a minute and then said, "You the main dawg, Herbert. You the man! I ain't forgetting any of this."

"Nor will I," Shark said happily. "Now, who's the man?"

"You are!" Eddie screamed with glee.

"Who's the man?" Shark asked again.

"You are!" Eddie repeated as he saluted Waters happily and took off.

Shark looked on with an evil smile. He had Eddie wrapped around his stubby little finger now. Once everyone signed the contracts, it would all be over. And any steps that Slamm Dunkk planned to use to thwart Shark's actions would hardly matter at all. He didn't have a chance of "saving" Eddie. The moment the poor unsuspecting Eddie Holder signed his name to the contract, he would belong to Shark Waters forever or until there was no use for the boy, whichever came first.

CHAPTER 8

Out of Control

Eddie was on an all-time high. His excitement about the car—but more so, the prospect of signing that contract—led him to drive to Alicia's house. Although there was going to be a party held in his honor the following night, he wanted to spend some quality time with Alicia and have a pre-celebration with her. His plan was to have a nice romantic dinner with her in an extravagant restaurant in the marina and sweep her off her feet. Besides, he could afford it; he had ten new Benjamin Franklin bills in his wallet. The challenge was, however, getting Alicia to warm up to him. He knew that Alicia was a bit upset with him, but once Alicia saw the car and he told her everything that was about to happen, all her disappointment and anger would melt away; he was sure of it. She would be like putty in his hands.

Eddie ran up the doorway and rang the doorbell eagerly. Alicia opened the door right away.

"Eddie?" Alicia was a bit surprised to see Eddie at her doorstep.

"I know we had a fight the other day and you're ticked off." Eddie wasn't planning on apologizing to Alicia for his behavior, but he wanted to be with her. "You doing anything now?"

"Not really," Alicia said abruptly. "Richie called awhile ago, looking for you. He said that he had talk to you. It sounded pretty important."

He wasn't going to let that twerp, Richie, spoil his moment with Alicia, but he knew that if he started insulting Richie, that would be the end of it. He maintained his cool and shot Alicia a big, charming smile.

Eddie shrugged his shoulders. "Whatever Richie has to say to me could wait. I got some really great news to tell ya, Al."

"Eddie, you better go talk to him or someone on the team," Alicia said with great concern.

"Look, I'm just trying to spend some time with my girl tonight. Why you gotta make such a big deal about me talking to Richie." Eddie could feel the anger rising, but he had to play it calmly. "There are more important things to me right now. Like this..."

Eddie pulled out the car keys and jingled them in front of Alicia in the same manner as Waters had done.

"I got me a car," Eddie announced, pointing to the 350Z parked at the curbside.

Alicia's eyes opened wide in amazement. "Where did you get that?"

"Remember the agent friend that I told you about? He lent it to me for a day."

Alicia shook her head. "What's the catch?"

"No catch," Eddie said, still trying to be charming although it was getting harder by the second with her attitude. "He's letting me drive it, and I was gonna tell you this over dinner, but I guess I should tell you now. I'm signing a contract tomorrow, and we're gonna parteee..."

Eddie grabbed Alicia's wrist gently and started swiveling his hips, doing a little dance. "What do you say, babe? C'mon, Al, let's go have some fun tonight."

"Are you crazy?" Alicia's voice was loud with both concern and agitation. "Eddie, do you know what you're doing? Don't you think all this going professional talk is happening too fast?"

"Whadda ya talking about?" Eddie spurted out, totally angry now. Just who was this girl to rain on his parade? "I don't know why you got your panties in a bunch, but you should be happy for me, not dissing me."

"I don't know, Eddie. You're so different now. I heard about what happened in practice today, and I don't know what to think anymore. I don't think I want to be with you anymore."

"You mean that?"

"Yes, I do!" She pulled her wrist away and slammed the front door, leaving Eddie all alone on the porch.

"Her loss, not mine," Eddie muttered, not feeling one bit of regret, under his breath to himself.

Eddie wasn't about to waste the gift that Herbert had given him for the day. If Eddie couldn't show off in front of his girlfriend, then he thought he could, at least, parade around in front of the guys, Richie, Sam and Flash, who would be hanging out at Vito's Pizza after practice. If he showed off the fancy car—maybe let them ride in it—and told them about the contract signing party tomorrow, it would shut all the guys up forever, and he would wind up being the talk of the team. *Yeah, Eddie is good enough to go pro. Maybe we were all wrong about him. We need him on the team more than ever. We owe him an apology.* The thought of it gave Eddie goose bumps. And as he strutted confidently toward the tables outside Vito's with his chest sticking out and his arms swinging heroically, he couldn't help but think the guys would gush all over him and treat him like some famous rock star.

"Yo, dawgs!" Eddie greeted pleasantly, noticing only Sam and Flash sitting at their round table. "I got some sweet news!"

Sam and Flash looked up and nodded their heads at Eddie. Sam had a dour expression on his face, while Flash frowned behind his sunglasses. Were they not happy to see the future megastar? And where was Richie? For some reason, he wanted to show off to Richie the most.

Giving the guys a hi-five each, Eddie grabbed and sat next to Flash. "Whassup?"

Flash turned away, and Sam looked down, but Eddie didn't really notice their body language at all. He was too far into his own world.

"Like I said, I got some sweet news." Eddie thumped his chest. "I'm signing me a contract tomorrow. And y'all are invited to my party tomorrow night."

Flash pushed his sunglasses up to his forehead and looked directly into Eddie's face. "You haven't heard, have you?"

"Whatcha talking about?"

Sam said, "You haven't talked to Richie, huh? He was looking for you."

"Why's everybody so interested in me talking to Sykes? Man, I got the most dope news in my whole life, and everybody wants to know if I talked to Richie Sykes. I don't get it!"

"You got kicked off the team, man," Flash said disappointedly. "That's what Richie wanted to talk to you about."

"You just playing with me," Eddie said, laughing a bit.

Shaking his head, Sam said, "It's true, Ed. After practice, we had a big discussion with coach, and the team decided to let you go."

"Okay, dawgs, joke's over," Eddie said, not wanting to believe the story. "You coming to my party or not? You my boys, so I want you guys partying with me."

Sam said, "You don't get it, do you? You're off the team."

Eddie looked down for a minute. He couldn't believe what was happening; he was the star of the team, and yet he was spat out and kicked to the curb just like common trash.

"It was a team decision. There was nothing we could do." Sam shook his head. "Look, I know we haven't been getting along, but we fought for you. Especially Richie. He's probably taking it the hardest."

Eddie erupted, "Yeah, and I suppose you guys said if Eddie Holder don't play, then we don't play, either."

"Hey, we said we fought for you. What more do you want?" Flash said strongly. "We done the best we could for you, but you dug your own freakin' grave, dawg!"

Looking down, Eddie gripped the edge of the table and began to shake intensely. He could hear Flash yapping away like a chihuahua, but he wasn't listening. Something so foreign and evil seemed to take over his entire body, and without any warning at all, he leaped off his seat and grabbed Flash, pulling him up and shoving him into a nearby stone pillar.

"Hey!" Flash screamed in surprise.

Flash tried to pry loose, but Eddie had his body pinned against the pillar with his left forearm tucked tightly under his neck, so that Flash couldn't breathe.

Eddie snarled like a wild beast, and as he lifted his right fist to strike the point guard, a raging, inner voice screamed out, *"Do it! Wipe him out! He deserves it!"*

And it jolted Eddie back. The voice was so menacing and overpowering, it frightened him. Taking a couple of steps back gingerly, he lowered his fist and released Flash, who crumpled to the ground and coughed violently.

Eddie stared at his hands in horror as if there were blood on them. He couldn't believe what he had just done to Flash, and all at once, he felt so incredibly remorseful. He had been angry before but never to the point of losing this much self-control. This was the first time that he had become so savage and violent, letting loose all his raw and animalistic emotions like the opening of floodgates. Yet, to Eddie, it seemed as if someone was pulling the strings and making him react. It was all very bizarre.

"What's wrong with you, Ed?" Sam yelled angrily as he helped Flash up.

"I don't know," Eddie uttered, "I'm sorry. I didn't mean to…"

Without finishing his sentence, Eddie, unable to face Sam and Flash any longer, suddenly turned and burst away, wondering what was going on inside his head.

Eddie came home a little after six o'clock in the evening. He parked the car about a half a block away from his own home, knowing that if his parents saw him get out of the car, he would have to explain his whole deal with Shark Waters. And right now, after all that had happened to him today, he wasn't in the mood to explain.

He had his own demons to deal with. It bothered him that he had lost control like that with Flash. Why did he attack him so brutally? Eddie had no answer; it just wasn't like him, yet it had happened, and there was nothing he could do about it now. Even a heartfelt apology wouldn't make things any better. It left a huge, burning hole in his heart, and the pleasant memory at the seaside restaurant with Waters seemed so distant.

What should have been an overwhelmingly amazing day for Eddie wasn't. Not only did he almost beat up a friend, but he was also kicked off the basketball team. He kept reliving every single moment of the day—back and forth, back and forth—like windshield wipers on maximum speed, and he still couldn't understand how things could go so haywire in so short a time span. By the time he stepped into the Holder household, he was totally numb. If only he could close his eyes and make things magically disappear…

Sighing deeply as he put his backpack down, he heard loud murmurs from the kitchen. It sounded like a fight between his mom and Aaron. He stood there for a moment, trying to make out the conversation.

"Go to your room and think about it!" This time his mom's voice was loud and clear.

Soon after, Eddie saw Aaron passing through the living room from the kitchen with his head down miserably.

"Wud up, little man?" Eddie greeted.

"What? Oh, hi, Eddie." Aaron's voice was quite sad.

"Sounds like you were getting chewed out by mom."

"Yeah, mommy said that I'm grounded because I play my Gameboy too much. Now I can't go to basketball day camp tomorrow."

"Yeah?" Eddie asked, feeling sorry for Aaron.

"Eddie, is that you?" Mom's voice boomed from the kitchen suddenly. "You get in here this instant!"

"In a minute, mom," Eddie said loudly.

"Now!" The voice belonged to his dad, which surprised Eddie a bit. He thought that it was just his mom in the kitchen.

He didn't know why his parents wanted to talk to him so urgently, but from the sounds of their voices, he gathered that it wasn't anything good.

Great...just great. All I need is more grief...

Eddie looked back to his little brother, who was crying now. "I gotta go. I'll be by to see ya later. Just hang in there."

Patting Aaron's head, Eddie went into the kitchen to face the music. Both his mom and dad were sitting at the kitchen table, and both had the same expression: grim.

"You forgot, didn't you?" his mom accused right away.

"Forgot what?" Eddie was dumbfounded. "Hey, I took the trash out last night."

"Young man, I asked you yesterday to pick up your little brother from school today. When I ask you to do something, I expect it to be done."

"Oh...sorry. Mom, I totally forgot." Eddie had completely forgotten about Aaron. "I had things to do."

Finally, dad spoke. "Like what, Edward? Do you mind telling us?"

Eddie felt badly enough, but he couldn't figure out why his parents were making such a federal case out of it. It was a simple mistake that only needed an apology.

"Stuff, pops. Stuff you and mom wouldn't understand." Eddie wasn't even sure if he understood it himself.

"Oh, we understand." Dad's voice was still low but very firm. "We understand that you've been thrown off the basketball team because of your antics."

Eddie exploded, "I can't believe that loser, Sykes, shot his mouth off. What's he doing? Going around the whole town and telling everybody about me? He must be getting his jollies talking smack. Dat's so whack!"

"Richie didn't tell us a thing," Mom said. "Your coach called and told us all about it. Honestly, Eddie, I don't know why you're always attacking Richie. He's such a good friend."

Ignoring the comment about Richie, Eddie looked away and muttered, "Well, I bet you're happy now that I can't play basketball."

"That comment's entirely uncalled for," Dad said. "However, I can't say that I'm unhappy that you're off the team. Maybe now, you'll concentrate on your schooling."

Eddie rolled his eyes.

"Don't you roll your eyes at me, boy!" Dad said loudly.

"What do you want me to do? Be all happy about it?" Eddie gave his parents a stern look. "Why's everybody gotta get in my face about basketball?"

Mom gave Eddie a sympathetic look. "I know it hurts right now and you're angry, but sooner or later, you'll realize that getting thrown off the team was a blessing in disguise. I know I sound like a broken record, but you have to start thinking about college."

"And if I don't? Whatcha gonna do?"

Dad shook his head. "As long as you live under our roof, you will do as we say. That's final."

"That's just total bullshh…"

"Don't you dare say that word in front of us," Mom warned, holding up a finger. "Why can't you understand that we're protecting you because we love you?"

"You just messing my life up!" Eddie yelled out.

"Well, I got news for you, people." Eddie opened and closed his hands quickly two or three times. "Eddie Holder's gonna play basketball and ain't nobody gonna stop me!"

"What's that supposed to mean?" Dad asked angrily.

Eddie had promised Herbert Waters that he wasn't going to utter a single word about him, but he had to tell them now. It would be the only way to make them understand that he truly had the talent and skills in basketball to go all the way.

"Exactly what I said," Eddie said in a harsh tone.

"You will not continue this nonsense any longer, Edward!"

"Hear me out, pop." Eddie's voice softened a bit. The mere thought of Herbert Waters seemed to calm Eddie down. "Please…"

With a frown, Dad crossed his arms. He sighed deeply and then said, "Don't know why I should, but go on."

"Mom, remember a guy named Herbert Waters who called the other day?"

"Name rings a bell," Mom said, nodding her head. "You said that he was connected to the school."

"Well, he ain't." Eddie paused for a moment, gathering himself. "He's my agent and I'm gonna sign with him."

Dad stood up angrily. "Are you insane, boy?"

Mom couldn't agree more with Dad, but she tapped his arm lightly. "Earl, give the boy a chance."

Dad sat back down and massaged his temples with his eyes closed.

"Hey, can I continue?" Eddie asked disrespectfully.

Dad opened his eyes and looked at Eddie with disappointment. "Go on."

"Ever since last year, he's been kinda following me around. Met with him today, and he wants me to sign a contract with him tomorrow."

Dad was totally perplexed. He gave him a "what-in-the-dickens-are-you-talking about" sort of look. This agent business was totally out of left field, and Dad didn't like it one bit. As much as he wanted to just ream Eddie another one, he knew that the fair thing to do was to hear the boy out, no matter how absurd it was.

Eddie continued, knowing that he hadn't convinced his parents one bit about his plans. "Herbert Waters is a real great dawg. You'd really like him. He told me that I can go pro, no sweat. He's got my back, and me and him are gonna go a long way."

"Eddie, we haven't even met the man, and you're acting like it's a done deal," Mom said.

"It is a done deal!" Eddie exclaimed.

"But what about your education, Eddie?" Mom asked in a stern voice. Now she was angry. What was her boy thinking? Obviously, not much.

"Don't worry about an education!" Eddie shot back agitatedly. "I'll get one in Europe."

Mom raised her eyebrows in disbelief. "Europe?"

"Yeah, Europe. I can finish my high school education in Europe after this year."

The boy had really fallen off the deep end!

In as calm a voice as possible, Dad said, "I want the number to this Herbert Waters, and we're going to put an end to your association with him once and for all."

"No, you won't!" Eddie's voice rose higher in pitch. "You don't own me! Man, why can't you understand that this is what I want?"

"Because it's crazy talk." Dad took a deep breath. "Get a grip on reality, boy. You're not ready for this, physically or mentally!"

"What? You don't think I can do this?"

"No, I don't. Look at the way you're acting now." Dad took another deep breath. "Eddie, what are you going to do when something that you don't like happens? Are you going to blow up every single time when you can't get your way? That's not the way of the world."

"Eddie, you will finish high school here. You will not go to Europe to get an education, and you will not play basketball. That's final!"

"WHY ARE YOU DOING THIS TO ME?"

Eddie pounded on the table in frustration. His rage had reached a boiling point; his whole body was shaking uncontrollably, and his breathing was quite shallow.

"Eddie, let's talk this through," Mom said soothingly. "We really want to help."

And then she reached over to put her hand on Eddie's shoulder to calm him down, but Eddie went berserk. He swatted her hand away brutally like a gnat. Then he got up and upended the table.

Reacting as quickly as he could, Dad went toward his son, but Eddie quickly backpedaled a couple of steps.

He pointed at his dad and shrieked, "Don't you touch me, old man!"

"Or you'll what?"

Eddie snarled with so much loathing and venom, "Or I'll drop you."

Dad moved cautiously closer to Eddie as he whispered, "Eddie, you need to calm down…"

"I don't need you! I don't need any of this!"

Like a madman totally out of control, Eddie bent over, grabbed the chair he had been sitting on and hurled it at a huge window while shouting the worst profanity a child could ever use against his parents. On impact, the chair shattered the window, and the window exploded with chucks of glass spraying the room. Dad lunged forward and quickly shielded his wife, the pieces of glass raining down on them.

He squinted at Eddie and saw a look of rampant fury in his son's eyes. This was clearly not the son that he knew. "Why, Eddie?"

Standing over them, Eddie was about to shout more obscenities at his parents when he heard a tiny voice say, "Eddie, no."

Eddie looked to his left and saw a horrified Aaron standing in the doorway with his hand to his mouth. There were tears streaming down his cheeks.

"No, Eddie, no…" Aaron whispered.

Eddie stood motionless for a minute, not knowing what to do. He darted his eyes from his parents and then back to Aaron. Eddie's lower lip began to quiver, and, he, too, began to sob like his little brother. Had Aaron not been standing there, who knew what Eddie was capable of doing next?

Taking a deep breath, Eddie covered his face with his hands. The place was eerily quiet, and all Eddie heard was his raging heart beating fiercely. *Thumpthumpthumpthumpthumpthump…*

After a long moment, he finally lowered his hands and viewed the shambles around him. Table upturned, a chair broken into pieces, glasses spewed all over the place, and his parents kneeling over, staring at him in ultimate shock. He couldn't believe this was all his doing. But, was it really?

Eddie felt a tug at his pant leg, and he looked down at Aaron, who had a very lost look on his face. Eddie wanted to hold him and tell him that everything was going to be okay. But he knew it wasn't. Not now, anyway. Maybe, not ever.

He stared at Aaron for a second. And then, without a word, he ran from the kitchen and stormed out the house, screaming like a raving lunatic.

CHAPTER 9

The Spirits of Basketball Present

What is wrong with me? I should be the happiest guy on the earth right now, but I can't even hold it together for one minute...

With some sunlight still left in the day, Eddie sat on the cool white sand, staring out at the Pacific Ocean blankly. He just had another major blowout, this time, with his parents, and Eddie just couldn't understand why he wasn't able to hold his emotions in check. Harsh words were one thing, but to become physical was another matter entirely. Never before in his life had Eddie ever touched his mother like that or behaved violently with his parents. And just knowing that Aaron witnessed the whole ugly incident made Eddie feel like such a...Well, there simply weren't enough suitable words to explain how he felt.

All of what was occurring just didn't add up. It didn't make any sense to him at all. His rash actions were one riddle after another. He couldn't quite comprehend why he was acting the way he was, but there was one thing he was absolutely sure of, as he tried to sort out the whole entire mess: his problems stemmed from what he yearned for the most.

But, I wanna play basketball so bad...

Teetering back and forth, Eddie was more confused than ever. On the one hand, there was Herbert Waters who was so high on him. But, on the other hand, everybody else was against him pursuing his hoop dreams

Eddie felt a moment of weakness. Maybe it wasn't in the cards for him to play basketball. He loved basketball to death—or so he thought—but did it mean that he had to make an enemy out of everybody? Was it really worth the trouble to lose everybody that he once held so close and dear?

But, I wanna play basketball so bad…

Eddie buried his face in utter frustration. He kept thinking about the past that the Spirits had forcefully shown him. Those days were so simple: No hang-ups, no fights, and no ego trip. Perhaps it would have been easier to just throw in the towel and go back to the easier life…to go back to the Eddie Holder who was happy, encouraging and caring. But had he reached a point of no return? Could he go back and become the "past" Eddie again?

But, I wanna play basketball so bad…

Too much thinking drained Eddie. He felt like his head was about to explode. He needed to "not" think about it for a while and try to enjoy what was left of the sun. Maybe the answers would come to him gradually when he wasn't agonizing so much about it.

Yes, I wanna play basketball so bad…

Eddie decided to lie down on the sand, but the moment he did, he almost jumped out his skin, his heart racing a million miles.

"Wud da?" Eddie asked puzzlingly, as he stood up and glared down at Slamm Dunkk, who had just suddenly appeared out of nowhere. "You, again?"

Spinning a basketball in his hand expertly, Slamm Dunkk chuckled at Eddie. "In the flesh."

Eddie stared at Slamm Dunkk with strong hatred. How could anyone be so laidback when he was having such a difficult time?

"Oh, Edward, Edward, Edward, what a tangled web we've weaved. You want to play basketball professionally, but no one is supporting you and that makes you lash out at everybody. And then you feel so guilty because you're hurting everyone around you." Slamm Dunkk hit his own forehead lightly in mock frustration. "'DoIplaybasketball? NahIwon'tplaybasketball. ButIreallywanna-playbasketball. OhI'msotorn! Ijustdon'tknowwhattodowithmyself.'"

Mumbling "retard" under his breath, Eddie just turned and darted off. He didn't need this added aggravation right now. But that really didn't prevent Slamm Dunkk from quitting his harassment. The irritating Spirit got up and caught up to Eddie, walking stride for stride while magically bouncing the basketball on the sand. Eddie noticed this fascinating feat, but Slamm Dunkk was the enemy. He wasn't about to praise his skill. He looked the other way and eyed the pier in the distance.

"So, Edward, what are we gonna do now?"

Silence.

"Don't pretend that you didn't hear me."

Still more silence.

"Aw, Edward, don't hate me because I'm so beautiful."

Without a word, Eddie suddenly zoomed away toward the pier, figuring he could shake Slamm Dunkk there. He ran at breakneck speed for a quarter of a mile, never once turning back to look at Slamm Dunkk. And once he reached the edge of the pier, he stopped and looked around. There was no Slamm Dunkk anywhere. He had successfully dodged him, and Eddie bent over, with hands on knees, to catch his breath for a moment.

"You can run, but you can't hide."

Eddie slowly looked up and saw Slamm Dunkk right in front of him, spinning the basketball. And as usual, Slamm Dunkk had that same sly grin on his face with no signs of fatigue.

Reacting quickly, Eddie summoned all the energy that he could and burst away as fast he could, back toward his original spot on the beach. The 350Z was parked not too far from there, and if Eddie could get there fast enough, maybe he could make a quick getaway and leave Slamm Dunkk in the dust.

Within a matter of minutes, Eddie reached the car, breathing harder than ever and opening the car door.

"What took you so long?" Slamm Dunkk was sitting in the passenger seat, cradling the basketball.

Totally fatigued, Eddie fell to his knees in defeat. No matter how hard he tried to escape, Slamm Dunkk was always there to intercept him. Eddie felt like the Wolf in that one "Droopy" cartoon.

Slamm Dunkk winked at Eddie. "Come on in, Edwardo."

Having really no choice, Eddie got into the car and sat behind the wheel. "I hope you're happy."

"Happy about what?"

Eddie stared long and hard at Slamm Dunkk. "You really messed things up for me."

Eddie felt so much better blaming Slamm Dunkk for his current situation. It certainly seemed to lift a huge burden from his shoulders.

"Don't blame me," Slamm Dunkk said, "You're in this mess because of your own doing, or should I say, undoing. I'm trying to help you see straight. That's all."

"Herbert Waters is the only dawg whose got my back." Eddie mumbled.

"Yeah, and then some." Slamm Dunkk's voice took on a serious tone. "Do you know who or what he is? He'll destroy your whole life, and I want to prevent that."

"You ask me, you're making my life more miserable."

"Oh, Edward, Edward, Edward, if you could only see the truth." Slamm Dunkk frowned. "Life wouldn't be this difficult."

"My life ain't none of your business. Just leave me alone!" Eddie pointed at himself with his thumb. "Herbert Waters is gonna take me places."

"Is that what you think?" Slamm Dunkk shook his head disappointedly. "Wake up and smell the coffee, boy!"

Eddie could feel the uncontrollable rage consume him again. He was ready to pounce on Slamm Dunkk, but suddenly, the seatbelt wrapped around him like a boa constrictor and Eddie couldn't move a muscle. He tried to wiggle himself free, but the more he struggled, the tighter the seatbelt bound him. And worse yet, the seatbelt seemed to multiply every second, wrapping Eddie up like a mummy.

"Temper, temper, young man," Slamm Dunkk said as he wagged his finger at him.

And soon, the seatbelt—or the seatbelts—had totally buried Eddie up to his neck, making it harder for him to breathe. His heart pounding hard, Eddie looked at Slamm Dunkk with wide-eyed terror, as if pleading to be released.

Slamm Dunkk flashed that superior smile of his at Eddie. He waved at Eddie and then crossed his arms like a genie. Slamm Dunkk jerked his head down a couple of times, and just like that, Eddie popped off into nothingness, leaving the seatbelts in a heap on the driver's seat.

When Eddie reappeared, he found himself all alone and free from Slamm Dunkk's smothering seat belts. He literally thought he was going to die of suffocation, but now that he knew he wasn't in any more danger, Eddie felt a huge sense of relief and hungrily sucked in the fresh air.

His once racing heart now returning to normal, he scanned his environment closely. Fortunately, Slamm Dunkk was nowhere to be seen, and Eddie was glad to be rid of the annoying Spirit. Yet, at the same time, Eddie wondered why Slamm Dunkk had sent him here to this place: Aaron's elementary school, or more specifically, the schoolyard.

It was recess. The elementary school kids were climbing the monkey bars and chasing each other around the grounds, while others played dodge ball, hopscotch or tetherball. In one corner, there were some kids gathered around the basketball courts. Eddie spotted Aaron right away and wanted to go over to greet him, but he realized no one could see him so he stopped himself in his tracks and stood in place.

"Now, what am I supposed to do here?" Eddie gazed up toward the sky. "Yo, Slamm Dunkk, what's the major plan now?"

As if it were an answer to his question, two Spirits came flying down from the bright blue sky and landed in front of Eddie. To Eddie, these Spirits seemed much stronger, much bigger, and much more forceful than the Spirits of Basketball Past; it was as if these guys were tailor-made for the physical style of play in today's game and could literally gobble up the competition for breakfast. But, then again, maybe it was Eddie's imagination running wild again, being that one of the two Spirits, who sported an untrimmed beard and mustache, was giving him the once around with an awful frosty glare.

"So this is the runt that we're supposed to save, huh?" the bearded Spirit snarled, looking disappointedly down at Eddie as though he was an unappetizing and unsatisfying dish for dinner. "He doesn't look like much."

Dressed in purple warm-ups, the bearded one that spoke was every bit his massive 7-foot plus frame but seemed a whole lot larger. This Spirit, who had colossal feet, was built like a football linebacker or even a World Wrestling Federation wrestler, but for all Eddie knew, the Spirit could really have been a T-Rex disguised as a human; he definitely made Eddie comprehend the uneasy emotions Jack felt as he climbed frantically down the beanstalk with the golden goose. Only an ignorant fool would try to tangle with the giant, bearded one.

"Majoris, that maybe so, but we have to do our job," the other Spirit said.

He was perhaps only an inch shorter than Majoris, but he was much leaner, wearing black warm-ups. Whereas Majoris seemed like the bad cop, the other Spirit seemed more like the good cop with his good-natured but ever watchful eyes.

"We're the Spirits of Basketball Present. I'm Orion," the good cop Spirit said, introducing himself. "And this is Ursa Majoris."

"Ursa Majoris? What kind of screwy name is that?" Eddie couldn't stop himself from laughing out loud. But the moment he blurted out his words, he knew that he made a fatal mistake. Ursa Majoris came extremely close to Eddie and looked down at him. Way down. Eddie felt his hot breath, and almost immediately, he felt his knees wobble weakly.

"Look, little man, I don't take my name too lightly," Ursa Majoris growled. "And I don't take my job too lightly, either. Neither does Orion here."

Eddie swallowed loudly and did not bother to look up. He was beyond scared, and he could only imagine what Ursa Majoris could do to him with one of those enormous fingers.

"Okay, okay, I'm sorry," Eddie stammered, his voice trembling and knees knocking. "Wh-Wh-What am I doing here at Aaron's school?"

Taking a couple of steps back, Ursa Majoris smirked. "Go over to your brother and watch."

"Yeah, see how you've influenced his life," Orion said.

Still full of fear, Eddie tiptoed timidly by Ursa Majoris while eyeing him. Ursa Majoris suddenly lifted his arms up and gave a big menacing growl like a grizzly bear.

"Yahhh!" Eddie screamed and ran to his kid brother.

"You really shouldn't have done that, Majoris," Orion scolded teasingly.

"You're right," Ursa Majoris said agreeably. "I shouldn't have, but I couldn't resist."

He winked at Orion, and both of them laughed, knowing that they had one up on poor old Eddie.

Standing under the backboard, Eddie watched the little kids pick teams. Aaron hadn't been chosen yet. He was the last of the two remaining. The other kid was a bit chubby and wore very thick glasses.

"Pick Aaron, pick Aaron," Eddie whispered. "He's a great player."

"I pick Henry," one of the captains, who was African-American, said.

The other captain, a Japanese boy, said, "Ah, I wanted Henry."

"Hey, what's wrong with me?" Aaron asked. "You know I'm a good player. How come no one wants me?"

The African-American captain said, "Because of your brother and how you play."

Eddie shouted, "What a buncha losers!"

He wanted to defend his younger brother, and he started to walk toward them until he heard Orion's voice.

"You know they can't see you."

"Oh, yeah." Eddie took a step back and watched on in frustration.

Aaron claimed, "My brother's awesome. You better take that back."

The Japanese kid said, "Whatcha gonna do, Aaron? Get your brother? My brother says that Eddie's all talk now. He can beat your brother in basketball anytime!"

"No way!" Aaron exclaimed. "My brother's way better than yours."

"Yeah, yeah, yeah, tell it to the hand," the Japanese kid said, as he put his palm in front of Aaron's face. "Hey, why don't we just play 5 on 4?"

"I play better than all of you put together anyway, Akira." Aaron said.

"That's what you think!" Akira said. "We don't like to play with you anymore. When you get the ball, you don't even pass the ball."

Aaron disagreed, "I don't do that!"

All the kids yelled, "Yeah, you do."

"Go away, Aaron," the African-American captain said. "We don't want to play with you anymore."

Aaron almost burst into tears. "Well, you can't play basketball like the way my big bro showed me. You're just jealous because I'm better than all of you."

The African-American captain repeated, "Go away, Aaron."

Aaron rubbed his tearful eyes and ran off.

"Aaron!" Eddie tried to follow his kid brother. He hated to see his little brother so sad and angry.

"It's no use, Edward," Orion said. "You can't soothe him. It is what it is."

"But…"

Orion said gently, "Edward, we have other places to go."

"Let's go," Ursa Majoris said gruffly.

He waved his huge muscular arms in big circles, and then an orange-brown sphere glowed around them. Carrying the weight of the three, it floated above the ground momentarily, and then it zipped off toward the bright sun, disappearing into the sky.

"Well, here we are," Orion announced as the three of them landed on the basketball courts of El Camino Park next to the beach.

It was evening time and the sun was setting. It was a glorious sunset with the sky colored in bright oranges and purples. But it was all wasted on Eddie. He stared into the horizon, but nothing was registering in his brain. Everything was just a big haze. He felt sorry for Aaron, wondering if his behavior was really shaping Aaron's personality in a negative way.

"Penny for your thoughts," Orion offered.

"What?" Eddie was brought back to the present reality. "I'm sorry…I was thinking about something else."

"Did I just hear an apology?" Ursa Majoris put his hands on his cheeks in mock surprise. "Edward Holder apologizing? Will miracles never cease?"

"Cut it out," Eddie said quietly. "I'm not in the mood. I'm worried about my kid brother."

Ursa Majoris said coldly, "You should be, Edward. It's all your fault."

"And I suppose you didn't magically create any of this?" Eddie asked suspiciously. "Just trying to make my life miserable…"

"Of course not." Ursa Majoris put his huge hands on his hips.

Orion said, "Everything that you've witnessed so far is true. We can't magically create incidents."

Looking down with sadness, Eddie sighed a deep sigh. "Yeah, I guess you're right."

"C'mon, Edward, you're not done yet," Ursa Majoris boomed. "There's still more to be done here."

"Like what?" Eddie asked.

"See that kid over there," Ursa Majoris said, pointing toward the furthest basketball court. "You're going to play one-on-one with him."

Eddie squinted his eyes and recognized the kid who was playing. His eyes widened in shock.

"You want me to play Sykes?" Eddie asked excitedly. "This has got to be some kind of joke, right?"

Orion shrugged his shoulders. "I'm afraid it's not a joke, Edward. It's a Friday evening, and we're actually in 'real' time here."

"You know, the present," Ursa Majoris grumbled.

"I suppose I don't have much of a choice, do I?" Eddie sighed.

"Nope." Ursa Majoris shook his head emphatically.

"Well, hey, it don't matter anyway. I'll whip his butt in," Eddie bragged.

"Maybe," Orion said. "Now, go."

Eddie slowly walked over to the other end of the court and stood there, watching Richie play alone. Richie was so into it he didn't even know Eddie was watching.

Eddie's heart began to beat quickly, and his palms felt clammy. All this time, he had been critical of the team and how his teammates weren't pulling their weight—especially Richie—and now, just as he was about to play a game of one-on-one with him, he wasn't quite so sure of himself. Suddenly Eddie's confidence was wavering. *What if I lose? What will Herbert Waters think? I'll blow my chance of becoming a pro…*

Unsure of what to do, Eddie turned back toward the Spirits, and impatiently, Ursa Majoris waved his huge hand, as if to say hurry up and play.

You can do this, Holder. Stop thinking that you're going to lose. You can beat Sykes with no problem. Eddie took a long deep breath.

"Hey, Sykes," Eddie said, using a deeply serious tone of voice.

Richie stopped playing and turned to Eddie. Right away, he gave Eddie a sympathetic look. "Hey, Eddie, how's it going? You heard, right?"

Eddie tried to shrug it off as much as possible, but he knew Richie was referring to him getting kicked off the team. "Don't matter none."

"Hey, I'm really sorry. You know, I looked for you all over the place to tell you what was going down, but you were nowhere. Where were you all this time?"

"I said, it don't matter," Eddie grumbled. "Let's just play some ball."

"You want to play b-ball with me?" Richie was a bit stunned.

"Yeah, I've been told to play one-on-one with you," Eddie replied without expression.

"By whom?"

"Those guys over there." Eddie jerked his thumb over his shoulder.

"Who?" Richie said when he looked over Eddie's shoulder.

Eddie turned around. The Spirits were gone, nowhere in sight.

"They were here a minute ago," Eddie said in puzzlement.

"Eddie, what's with you lately? You've been acting really goofy lately."

"Never mind," Eddie said. "C'mon, let's go!"

"Okay, if you say so," Richie said, unsure of what to do.

"Winner's outs."

Eddie picked up the ball from the ground and was ready to pass the ball to Richie, but noticed the hesitant look on Richie's face. "Now what?"

Richie said, "I feel real bad about what happened."

"Never mind. Let's play some hoops." Eddie wanted to forget everything and get on with the game. He would show the Spirits—wherever they were—they were making a big mistake by forcing him to play basketball against Richie Sykes. And once he did defeat Sykes easily, Eddie would feel some sort of redemption.

"You can take it out," Richie said. "Age before beauty."

"Funny, Sykes," Eddie said with a big grin. "Very funny."

At the half court line, Eddie said, "Check the ball."

He passed it to Richie hard. Richie caught it easily and returned it right back to Eddie.

"Okay, let's go!"

Eddie dribbled the ball slowly as he crossed the half-court line. In his defensive stance, Richie was hunched in front of Eddie, and as Eddie drove to his left, Richie stuck with him. Then Eddie quickly did a 360-degree spin to reverse his position and went to his right. This move faked Richie out and Eddie had a free lane to the basket.

When Eddie tried to lay the ball up and into the basket, Richie came running in from out of nowhere, blocking the shot off the backboard and recovering it. In disbelief, Eddie stood frozen as Richie dribbled the ball out past the 3-point line.

"C'mon," Richie said.

As Eddie came charging at Richie, he released a jump shot outside the 3-point line. The ball went up in a perfect arc and swished into the basket. Nothing but net!

Richie took the ball. He dribbled the ball inbounds with Eddie guarding him, but unlike Eddie, Richie made no fancy moves. He simply dribbled to his right, passing Eddie with no difficulties and laid the ball up and into the basket with ease.

"That's three," Richie said. "You sure it's okay with winner's out?"

"Yeah, it's fine," Eddie said in agitation.

Once again, Richie took the ball out. He dribbled the ball slowly and deliberately, stopping at the top of the key. With Eddie guarding him very closely like white on rice, Richie feigned to his left, but Eddie didn't take the bait. Then Richie feigned to his right. Again, Eddie didn't bite. Then, suddenly, Richie took a couple of swift steps back from Eddie and launched another three pointer. The result was the same as before. The ball swished through the net, and just like that, it was five to zero in Richie's favor.

"Wanna take a quick break?" Richie asked pleasantly.

Eddie was angry at himself. How was this possible? He knew that Richie was a good player—although he would never admit it publicly—but was he that much better than Eddie? Was this the same kid who cried when he couldn't make the varsity team as a freshman? Did a year make that much of a difference?

Eddie tried to shake his negative thoughts away. Sure, it didn't help that Eddie was pre-occupied with Aaron, but that shouldn't have mattered. It was just pure dumb luck that Richie made the first three baskets. Pounding his chest to pump himself up, Eddie became determined to beat Richie. He would see to that. He would defeat Richie to a pulp.

"Bring it on, Richie," Eddie said sharply. "You ain't see nothing yet."

They had played three more games, and the results were the same. Richie won all three games effortlessly with Eddie scoring no more than five points in each game. Richie's every move made Eddie look like an elementary school student playing against a college student. Eddie used all his tricks in the book, but it didn't faze Richie at all. Practically every single time, Richie found an answer to score a basket or block one of Eddie's shots. No matter how hard Eddie had tried, he was simply no match for Richie. There was nothing flashy about Richie; he just had sound basketball fundamentals, and Eddie just couldn't figure out what had gone wrong.

An exhausted Eddie sat against the basketball stanchion. He was almost in tears after being defeated three straight games.

"Ah, come on, Eddie," Richie said softly. "You're just having an off-day, man. And I know you're hurting about the team, too."

Wiping the tears away, Eddie looked at Richie. "Do you know who I am? I'm Eddie Holder."

"Yeah, Eddie Holder," Richie muttered under his breath. "I almost forgot."

Eddie stood up. "This stuff is not supposed to happen to me. I'm Eddie Holder, future superstar, but I can't even beat a sorry little sophomore."

Richie felt guilty about beating Eddie so easily, and he didn't know how to comfort Eddie in his misery. Yet, at the same time, he couldn't bear to watch how pathetically Eddie handled his defeat.

"Eddie, I have to go home," Richie said.

"Let's play one more game," Eddie exclaimed wildly. "Just one game, and I'll show you that I'm better. I was just giving you a chance to make you feel good."

Somehow, Richie didn't think so. "Sorry, I have to go home. It's getting late."

"What, you chicken?" Tears started rolling down Eddie's face again.

"I'll see you around," Richie said.

He gathered his basketball and walked away.

Eddie screamed at the top of his lungs, "Don't walk away from me. We ain't finished yet."

Richie heard Eddie's words but continued to walk away without looking back.

Eddie screamed again, "Come back. You can't do this to me!"

Knowing that it was no use, Eddie sank to his knees in defeat. He buried his face into his hands and sobbed loudly for a minute. As he cried, he felt a hand land on his shoulder.

"Edward, time to go home," Orion said.

It wasn't as if he didn't hear Orion, but the tears just kept flowing from his eyes uncontrollably, and at the moment, crying was about the only thing he was capable of doing.

CHAPTER 10

Surprises Galore

The early morning sun blazed down on Eddie, and Eddie opened his eyes suddenly, jerking his body up from the sand. Totally disoriented, he looked around him and saw that he was at the beach. His body drenched in sweat and his heart pounding, the last thing he remembered vividly was getting wrapped up in a sea of seatbelts and then everything going blank. He couldn't remember what had happened after the fact, but it felt like some major pieces of the jigsaw puzzle were missing. Then it came to him in a flash; he remembered his nightmare: Richie beating him in one-on-one and his brother being picked on by his peers.

But, was it really a nightmare? Everything seemed so real.

And then Eddie saw it. The basketball that Slamm Dunkk had been playing with was right next to him, and Eddie knew instantly that whatever he saw in his so-called nightmare actually happened.

Aaron!

Without a thought, he stood up and ran to the 350Z. His only concern was Aaron right now. If his behavior was really influencing Aaron, then he needed to talk to his little brother and fix the problem. How could he be so blind and not see that Aaron idolized him while imitating Eddie's every move? From his eating habits to breaking rules to defying their parents.

What have I done?

As Eddie raced through the empty streets toward his home, all sorts of images exploded in his mind; he saw happy images and sad images; pleasant images and disturbing images; he saw images of Aaron, Richie, Sam, Flash and his parents; he saw himself studying with Alicia in the library; he saw himself fighting with Alicia in the hallway at school; he saw the coach and Byron Thompson and his elementary school teacher, Miss Lane; he saw Herbert Waters, Slamm Dunkk and the Spirits that had come to visit him.

And, suddenly out of nowhere, it dawned on him like the brightest nova in the galaxy that he had been wrong about everything. He needed to make changes. He would make things right with everybody.

Eddie smiled to himself as he parked the 350Z in front of his house. He didn't have to hide the car from his parents anymore. From now on, he was going to be straightforward and honest about everything. He wasn't going to create any more drama for anybody. He was going to be the old, sweet Eddie, whom everybody loved. And just the mere idea of that rejuvenated him. It was going to be totally different ball game, effective immediately.

Eddie got out of the car and strolled up the walkway confidently. He was going to talk to his little brother and then apologize to his parents for his terrible behavior. He was going to gain their trust again and be that son they were always proud of.

"Eddie?" a voice called from above.

Eddie looked up and to his right to see who had called out his name. It was Richie, and he was standing next to an open window in his bedroom next door.

"Where have you been?' Richie asked politely.

Eddie stared blankly at Richie. The sight of Richie served as a remembrance of everything that had gone bad yesterday: getting kicked off the team and losing so easily to him in one-on-one basketball. It truly pricked at Eddie's heart and pride. But he was starting over a new leaf.

Taking a really deep breath, Eddie said, "Why you asking, dawg?"

Richie hadn't been called "dawg" in such a long time; it made him wonder if things were straight with them now.

"Well, you never came home last night and your parents were so worried," Richie finally answered.

"Oh, yeah." It finally dawned on Eddie that he hadn't been home last night after his trying encounter with Slamm Dunkk. "Well, I better go talk to them. See ya."

Eddie was about to wave good-bye, but Richie called out again, "Eddie?"

"Yeah?"

"Hey, I'm sorry about yesterday. I know you had a lot of things on your mind. I know how good you are." Richie gave Eddie a wan smile. "Are we okay now?"

Eddie returned the smile, and just as he was about to say something reassuring, the front door opened. Casually, he glanced quickly at the door and saw his mom; just behind her was Herbert Waters.

Herbert Waters? What's he doing here?

For one minuscule second, Eddie made direct eye contact with Waters, and then, without warning, a strong surge jolted through Eddie like a powerful locomotive. And everything that Eddie had set out to do initially vanished from his mind completely. Slowly, an evil smile crept across Eddie's face.

"So, we okay?" Richie asked again.

"When were we ever okay?" Eddie snarled at the startled Richie. Whatever tenderness Eddie had shown just earlier had totally evaporated into thin air. It was as if that quality had never existed. "You got lucky last night! Next time we play, ain't no way you gonna win 'cuz I'm the king of the courts! Na mean?"

"Eddie!" his mother shouted from the door. "Where are your manners?"

Eddie rolled his eyes. He knew he was going to get an earful from his mom, but he wasn't worried. Nor did he really care. Herbert Waters had his back.

"Edward Holder, you get in here this instant," Mom demanded. "You have a guest."

"Okay, mom," Eddie said.

Eddie looked back up at Richie. Richie had an extremely disappointed look on his face, but Eddie didn't care. He saluted him with two fingers and coolly walked into the house.

"How are you doing, Eddie?" Waters said as he shook Eddie's hand. "How's the car handling?"

"It's great, man!" Eddie spread his arms out wide. "It's dope!"

"Isn't it wonderful that Mr. Waters lent you his car, Eddie?" Mom squealed.

"Huh?"

Mom said, "Well, since Eddie's back home, let's go back in, Mr. Waters. I'm sure my husband would love to hear more of your stories."

Mom skipped happily by Waters and Eddie, and Eddie gave Waters a confused look. He didn't get a look of warning or bewilderment from his mom when the car was mentioned. He didn't even get a chewing out for not coming home last night.

"What's going on?" Eddie whispered.

"I told you I would take care of everything." Waters winked at Eddie and went to join Eddie's parents in the living room as if he were part of the family.

Standing in the alcove, Eddie pondered this remarkable event for a minute and just didn't know what to make of it. He was extremely perplexed, but he went into the living room, anyway, to see what was awaiting him.

Waters was sitting in between his mom and dad, and to Eddie, it seemed like all three of them were old pals. His dad, especially, seemed overly jovial, which was definitely a sharp contrast to his mood yesterday.

"Hey, where's Aaron?" Eddie asked right away when he noticed his little brother was nowhere in sight.

With a smile, Mom answered, "He's at basketball camp, remember? But he'll be so thrilled when he gets home. Mr. Waters was generous enough to buy him a new X-Box system."

Eddie arched his eyebrows in bafflement. Just yesterday, his parents had grounded Aaron for playing too many videogames, but here they were reversing their word and acting like nothing had happened. He just didn't get it.

"Yeah, Ed, why didn't you tell us more about this great guy?" His dad slapped Waters' shoulder hard. "You know, if you had just explained a little bit more yesterday, your mom and I wouldn't have been so hard on you."

Eddie just nodded his head. The last time he had seen his dad in this kind of mood was when…Well, he'd never seen his father this happy, and it just seemed just way too bizarre.

"Ed, you have our blessing. If you want to pursue basketball, then go right on ahead. We've already signed that consent form." Dad punched Waters in the arm this time. "As long as Waters is behind you all the way, I won't say anything. And money is no object. No matter how much that program costs, I'll pay for it. But there is one condition, though."

There it was. Eddie knew it was too good to be true.

"What's that, pops?" Eddie said with a frown.

"Let me drive that 350Z this whole weekend." Dad held up a finger. "In fact, if you and Mr. Waters will allow me to take that beautiful car up the coast to Santa Barbara with your mom tomorrow, we have a deal. What do you say, Ed?"

Now, this was beginning to scare Eddie. This wasn't the same man who stood before him yesterday and threw down the gauntlet. This was some alien who had taken over his dad's body. It was something out of *Invasion of the Body Snatchers*. Was this real? Or was he dreaming? Did yesterday even happen for his parents? And, exactly, how did Waters persuade his parents to change their minds?

It wasn't that Eddie wasn't happy all of this was all coming into place for him, but his gut was telling him that it was all wrong instinctively. Worriedly, Eddie looked at Shark—who seemed just a tad fatter today—but the moment he looked into Shark's eyes, all his worries melted away instantaneously.

Don't fight this, kid. It's all right...

"Well, Ed? What do you say?"

"No problem, pops, be my guest," Eddie answered, "that is, if it's okay with Mr. Waters."

"No need to ask," Waters said. "We're all one big happy family."

"We certainly are," Dad agreed.

"Then it's settled. We're good to go." Waters was so close to victory he could almost taste it. "Normally, I'd like to keep the signing of the contract low-key, but this is how it's going to go down tonight. We'll have this gala festivity by the beach because it's so big! I'll invite some celebrities, athletes and maybe even some local networks. And then...POW! Eddie will sign the contract in front of thousands. Then it'll all be official."

Hearing all this, Eddie's heart began to pound rapidly, as he imagined himself the "roast" of the party with all these celebrities around him. It would be the most awesome event in his life!

"Dat's so coo," Eddie said. "But I got one favor to ask you."

"Anything, kiddo. Anything at all."

"I want some of my dawgs to be at my party. You know kinda show them that I'm the real thing." Eddie held up a finger. "But I don't want that retard, Sykes, showing up!"

Mr. Waters smiled. "No problem. It's done!"

Eddie slapped him a hi-five.

"Then I'll see you all tonight," Shark announced, getting up off the couch. "A limo will pick you up promptly at 5:30PM, so be ready."

Mom gave Waters a hug. "Well, the next time you come, you let us know in advance and I'll cook you a big meal."

Waters pecked a good-bye kiss on Mom's cheek.

"It's been a pleasure," Dad said.

Both Dad and Mom walked Shark to the door, and Eddie lay on the sofa with his hands behind his head confidently and closed his eyes. Last night had really taken a tow on him. He was a lot more fatigued than he realized, but it didn't change the fact that he was on his way to stardom. With eyes closed, he smiled to himself, as he heard an internal voice saying, *Go with the flow and everything will be perfect.*

"Not good," Slamm Dunkk uttered to himself as he watched Shark Waters stepping from the Holder household from across the street. "Not good at all." He had shot an airball with Eddie. Instead of concentrating on Eddie first, what Slamm Dunkk should have done was eliminate the competition. His first warning wasn't enough, and now, it looked like Shark Waters, who was much fatter than he was when Slamm Dunkk had first encountered him, was on the verge of taking Eddie Holder's soul completely. Taking on a transparent form, Slamm Dunkk had witnessed everything that had gone on in the house, and he realized Eddie had virtually reached a point of no return. This morning, there may have been a glimmer of hope just before Eddie had returned home, but now, he was "in too deep" since he had met with Shark again. And tonight, once Eddie signed that contract, everything would be loss and Waters would own Eddie.

Slamm Dunkk was angry with himself. He had taken Shark too lightly—he didn't seem like a challenge when they first met—and Shark had made an unexpected and intelligent move. Slamm Dunkk never saw it coming. Never did he once stop to think that Shark would go to Eddie's parents. Now, with Eddie's parents thoroughly convinced—a hex had obviously been put on them—it not only made Eddie believe that he could play ball professionally, but it also gave Shark that much more power over Eddie.

Slamm Dunkk watched Shark Waters enter a silver BMW 750i and drive off down the street. He had to do something about Shark before it was too late, but what? The Elders had not yet approved Shark's exile to another dimension, and Slamm Dunkk wasn't sure when it was going to happen. Maybe Shark was right. The Elders had never exiled another Spirit—present or former—to another dimension and were never going to. Ever.

He couldn't wait any more on the Elders. He was going to do something about Shark, and if he got into trouble later with the Elders, then so be it. He would deal with the consequences later. Eddie Holder's future was at stake, and at this instant, Slamm Dunkk had to drive to the hoop before the clock expired to 0:00.

Driving his Beemer, Shark Waters smiled smugly behind his cool Rayban sunglasses. He was so close to accomplishing his mission; he would be rich very soon. And it was such a piece of cake this time. The temporary hex he put on the Holders worked so well, he thought about milking it some more. The Holders were so loaded with dough, what would it matter if he tried to get some more money out of them? Besides, who was going to stop him?

Certainly not Slamm Dunkk. That Spirit turned out to be a joke, making such idle threats like that. Exile, indeed! None of his cheap parlor tricks seemed to have a long lasting effect on Eddie, and Waters wondered how in the world Slamm Dunkk could have become a Spirit in the first place? Sure, Waters was expelled from the Academy, but at least, he had honed his skills by himself to become more than capable. His success rate showed for it. Slamm Dunkk was no challenge for him. To Waters, Slamm Dunkk was like the twelfth man of a basketball team, who rarely got off the bench to play games except for garbage time.

With victory practically assured, Waters hummed happily as he drove along a winding road along the coast. It was fairly early on a Saturday morning, so there was hardly any traffic. Having no regard for safety, he drove down the middle of the twisting two-lane winding road at full speed, his car skidding dangerously. But Waters didn't care. He was invincible; he was the king of the Spirits. He was…in trouble!

As he came around a bend, the steering wheel locked up. Shark tried to step on the brakes, but the Beemer was going so fast, it skidded and crashed through the guardrail and drove off the cliff. Shark's eyes widened with fear as the car plummeted toward the ocean. But the car never crashed into the ocean! About ten feet away from making contact, the car abruptly froze in mid-air, and an orange-brown force field enveloped the car.

"What's going on here?"

"My, oh my, Herbert, how we've put on the weight!" a voice said from behind Shark.

Shark looked into his rearview mirror and saw Slamm Dunkk sitting in the backseat. He immediately turned his head to look at him.

Ignoring Slamm Dunkk's fat joke, Shark shouted deliriously, "You think this is going to stop me? You've got to be kidding!" Shark gave Slamm Dunkk an evil look. "Is this the best you got? Whatever happened to getting exiled to another dimension? Isn't going to happen, huh?"

Slamm Dunkk noticed how overly confident Shark was, but he had every right to be. Shark was winning the war.

"Maybe, I can't banish you yet, but at the very least, this will contain you until I can straighten out Eddie!"

"Holder's unreachable now!" Shark laughed loudly. "And tonight he'll be entirely mine."

"I can't let you do that!"

Shark looked out the car window and down below. He barely made out another Spirit—a huge Spirit—holding up the glowing sphere. Two against one, but it didn't seem to faze Shark one bit.

"And who's gonna stop me? You and that big gorilla down there? That's one big joke!"

Shark made a guttural laughing sound and shot his arms up toward the ceiling of the car. As his eyes flashed a brilliant red, fierce lightning bolts hurled up, tearing the roof of the car wide open. The bolts continued upward without losing any of its velocity or power and easily ripped the upper part of the sphere. Then, as rapidly as the bolts shot up, they flew down even faster.

With a forceful impact, the bolts shred the sphere and the Beemer apart, causing a violent explosion. Shards of glass and metal and pieces of the sphere scattered in a million different directions, raining into the ocean. The nearby cliffs swayed forward, and the surface of the water rippled ferociously.

And then, before long, it was calm and peaceful. The cliffs stopped rocking, and the ocean had calmed to a still, quietly lapping the bases of them. There was no trace of the car or the sphere. No sign of Slamm Dunkk. Nor the huge Spirit that Waters had dubbed "that big gorilla."

Standing by the guardrail that his Beemer had crashed through just moments ago, Shark stared at the quiet ocean glittering from the early morning sun. And he smiled to himself, silently claiming victory. Game over.

CHAPTER 11

On the Verge of a Nightmare

Just as Shark Waters had promised, the limousine had picked up Eddie and his parents and drove them to the private party. Eddie was a bit disappointed about Aaron not being able to attend, and he was sure that Aaron was probably just as disappointed. But Eddie promised himself that he would tell his little brother everything that happened, so much so, that it would be like Aaron was actually at the party.

Twisting up through the hills on the main drag of one of the more affluent residential areas, the limousine purred smoothly. It seemed like an eternity for Eddie, but the ride itself was only about thirty minutes long. And when the hill leveled off and the limousine headed straight toward a huge entrance of what looked to be a grand park, Eddie's heart pounded with excitement.

Looking through the window, Eddie could see this was definitely going to be one huge extravaganza. Two gigantic spotlights near the entrance gates shot upward, the shafts of lights dancing in the evening sky. A few television network vans were parked nearby with television reporters making their live on-air broadcasts. Eddie could also see droves of excited people awaiting his arrival with a cordon of security guards guarding the sacred red carpet, which seemed to lead into the park proper. Instantly, Eddie knew he had hit the big time. All this for a contract signing ceremony, and he hadn't even played ball professionally yet. This was definitely bigger than the Academy Awards!

The limousine finally came to a stop in front of the red carpet, and a burly security guard opened the door for the Holder family. First, Mom left the limousine, and then Dad. And when Eddie finally exited the limo, looking sharp in his black Armani suit, there was a thunderous roar from the already excited crowd. He blew kisses to the crowd, using both of his hands, and the crowd just went crazy. Eddie soaked it all in, enjoying the moment.

The security guard said, "Mr. Holder, if you will follow me."

Eddie nodded to the guard and made his way across the red carpet, walking like the king of the world who was about to greet his royal subjects.

The red carpet went into the park, and it ended at an extremely gigantic archway that seemed to be modeled after France's Arch of Triumph. The archway itself opened to an enormous cement courtyard that was the size of two basketball gyms.

Along the edges of the courtyard were tall palm trees that alternated with ten feet high ice sculptures of basketball players in various poses. The sculptures were, at once, dazzling and tasteful. In the center of the courtyard were several long rows of table that had platters of the finest foods and champagne. Most of the people—about one thousand or so, Eddie estimated—were gathered around the tables, eating and socializing. Just beyond the tables was a small parquet dance floor equipped with red and white strobe lights. There were some young people having a genuinely fun time as they shook their booties to the latest Beyoncé song blaring from the huge speakers placed on two corners of the dance floor.

Directly behind the dance floor and opposite the Holder family, at the far end of the courtyard, was a raised platform with a podium. It was there that Shark Waters in his gaudy pink tuxedo stood waiting for his star. Shark waved excitedly to Eddie, telling him to get on the stage.

Eddie looked at his parents. "My kingdom awaits!"

He embraced both his mom and dad and headed toward the platform. Eddie walked past the rows of tables and then crossed the dance floor. He noticed Sam, Flash and Alicia all grooving to the song, and they, in turn, noticed the man of the hour and approached him.

"Great party, Ed," Sam greeted as he shook Eddie's hand.

Flash hollered, "Yo, homie, this place is so dope! Thanks for inviting me."

Eddie nodded coolly, recognizing a nasty-looking welt on Flash's neck. He felt a tinge of guilt, but it didn't seem to matter to Flash. Flash was having such a fantastic time, Eddie wasn't about to mention yesterday's ugly incident, which seemed like eons ago.

"No problem, man. You guys are my boys!"

"I'm not your boy!" Alicia squealed. "I'm your woman!"

Alicia curled up to Eddie and blew him a kiss. Eddie smiled bashfully and gave her a kiss on the top of her head.

"Glad you're enjoying it," Eddie said happily. "Well, gotta go, dawgs. Have fun!"

Eddie walked off the dance floor and stepped up to the platform. Shark came to greet him. He had a huge wolfish smile on his face as he held up and shook what Eddie believed to be the contract.

"This is your magic moment," Shark hummed. "But before you put your John Hancock on it, I have another gift for you."

Casually reaching into his pants pocket, Shark produced a tiny jewelry box and handed it over to Eddie. Eddie immediately opened it up and saw a solid gold earring hoop.

"Dis is so gangsta! You the man, Herbert!"

Eddie attached the earring to his pierced earlobe carefully, smiling from ear to ear, and Shark felt another piece of Eddie's soul pulsating into his body. It was only a matter of seconds before he possessed Eddie entirely.

Shark patted Eddie on the shoulder. "It's showtime."

He put the contract on top of the podium and spoke into the microphone, "Excuse me, everybody. I think we'd like to start now."

The music and strobe lights immediately stopped, and the entire place erupted with loud cheers, literally rocking the courtyard. People pushed their way closer to the platform to get a better glimpse of the future mega superstar, Eddie Holder.

Eddie stepped forward to the podium. "Thank you all for coming tonight."

The crowd began to chant, "Eddie! Eddie! Eddie!"

Eddie raised his arms up triumphantly as the chants continued to grow louder and louder. He smiled and absorbed it all in, looking at the overzealous crowd. Feeling a bit like a cult leader, Eddie thought if it were going to be frenzied like this all the time, then he would learn to live with it. And absolutely love it…

Slamm Dunkk woke up dazed, sitting against some sort of strange rock formation. He didn't know how he got here or how long he had been out, but one thing was certain: it was one doozy of an explosion. Shark Waters had really done a number on them, and now, he definitely had the upper hand.

Wherever Slamm Dunkk was, it was dark, stifling and rancid, and he couldn't make out much around him. He was still aching from the blast, and the whole situation looked pretty bleak from his perspective.

He sat still for a moment, trying to gain his balance, and he noticed that his graduation cap, which was practically a permanent fixture, was amiss. He was about to raise his hand to his head but realized that he couldn't move his arms. For that matter, he couldn't even move any other muscle in his body. He was bound by invisible restraints. Definitely the mark of a Spirit and no doubt an evil one at that.

Slamm Dunkk would worry about the restraints later. For the moment, he had to figure out where he was and find a way out. He squinted his eyes and scanned the area—he certainly wasn't in Kansas anymore—and let his eyes adjust to the surrounding darkness. Just a few feet away from his right was a small mound of decomposed skulls, and mounted against the walls of rock were a few shackles, some with skeletons attached to them. In the middle of the chamber, there was a deep pit with deadly fumes wafting up toward the high ceiling.

Right away, he knew where he was. He was in a dimension dubbed the "Ghetto," where down and out Spirits, who no longer cared about saving others, dwelled with other non-human life forms that were just as miserable. The Ghetto was essentially a horrendous place to live with no hope whatsoever, and once inside the dimension, it was extremely difficult to get out. But Slamm Dunkk didn't panic—he had a mission to accomplish. He wasn't about to let a minor thing like this deter him. Once he got out of these restraints, he would go searching for his missing colleague, Ursa Majoris, and then they would escape from this dreadful dimension.

Chanting something under his breath, Slamm Dunkk tried to break out of the restraints, but he could not move. He chanted again, but still nothing. He tried again for a third time. The restraints hadn't budged a bit.

It seemed extremely laughable that he couldn't get out of something that seemed like mere child's play, but some energy force here was preventing him from using his Sorcery Arts power.

Slamm Dunkk took in a deep breath and summoned all his focus and concentration. He could feel the restraints loosening up slowly, and before long, he freed himself and struggled to his feet. He stretched out whatever kinks he had in his body and then searched for a way out.

Using both hands to feel his way through, he slinked along the rocky walls of the chamber to his left. He moved very slowly and carefully. And after a couple of minutes, he found a huge opening and peered into it. What Slamm Dunkk saw was a long tunnel that led to the outside. The distance from where he stood to the exit was, he figured, probably about the length of a football field.

Slamm Dunkk tried to make a run for it, but without warning, a huge paw grabbed the back of his neck and swung him back like a little rag doll. With full force, he slammed into a wall and slid down limply. Like a dazed boxer, Slamm Dunkk tried to get up from the mat, but the paw immediately slammed down on the top of his head with unbelievable force. He fell flat on his face, still conscious…barely.

Looking up, he was able to make out his attacker, and the sight was definitely not one of beauty. His attacker had the body of a gorilla, but its head was shaped like a hammerhead shark.

As the gorilla, or whatever it was, prepared to attack again, Slamm Dunkk rolled to his right, and by coincidence, he came across his graduation cap near the skulls. Immediately, he whipped his cap like a boomerang, and the cap hit the mid-section of the gorilla-shark. The creature howled in pain, holding its stomach.

Gathering as much energy as he could, Slamm Dunkk got up, scooped up his cap and headed for the opening, but the creature somehow grabbed a hold of his ankles and started swinging him around.

Slamm Dunkk didn't have the will to fight anymore. He was far too weak and too dizzy, and now he wanted to vomit his head off.

The creature held Slamm Dunkk's body above his head and headed toward the pit. And just as it was about to toss him down the pit, something miraculous happened. Out of nowhere, someone, or something, came storming in and tackled the gorilla-shark. Slamm Dunkk's body flew from the gorilla-shark's grasp and smashed into a wall.

Feeling like he just had gone a few rounds with Muhammad Ali, Slamm Dunkk tried to get up to make a run for it, but he was too groggy. He lay on the ground facedown and just listened to the all the grunting and smashing noises that went on behind him. If he was lucky, maybe both the gorilla-shark and this new intruder would knock each other out, and then he could make a run for it, that is, if he was able. But that would not be the case. The struggling sounds had all but ceased, and now, Slamm Dunkk heard heavy footsteps approaching.

As weak as he was, Slamm Dunkk readied himself to do battle again, but to his surprise, he heard a familiar voice calling, "Hey, Slamm."

Slamm Dunkk turned slowly around and looked up at Ursa Majoris. "Hi ya, buddy."

Ursa Majoris had a worried look on his face. "We have to get out of here quick. I don't know how long that thing is going to be out."

Slamm Dunkk dusted himself off and went to retrieve his cap, which was near the unconscious creature. He stared at it for a long while and then turned to look at Ursa Majoris.

"Hideous thing, isn't it?" Slamm Dunkk put his graduation cap back on and gave Ursa Majoris a dirty look. "Hey, what took you so long?"

"C'mon, Slamm, we have to get out of here."

"In a minute, in a minute," Slamm Dunkk said as he sat down against a wall, bringing his knees up to his chin.

"Slamm!"

Slamm Dunkk looked up at Ursa Majoris and smiled. "Hey, if it wakes up again, just knock it out again."

Ursa Majoris shrugged his massive shoulders. "I suppose."

"Hey, you have any powers?"

"A little bit. Why?" Ursa Majoris scratched the top of his bald head.

"We have to get out of here somehow, and do it together. Remember, we still have that big problem we haven't solved yet."

"Don't worry, I haven't forgotten," Ursa Majoris said with a grimace.

But Slamm Dunkk wasn't listening. His mind was back on Eddie. Once they were back in Eddie's world—and Slamm Dunkk had no doubt that they would be—he had to somehow get back on track with Eddie. It would, however, be an almost impossible task now that Eddie was nearly possessed by Shark. Nearly, but not entirely. Slamm Dunkk knew this to be the key to it all. If Eddie's heart wasn't totally tainted, then there had to be some way to get at whatever purity that remained in Eddie's heart and soul. But Slamm Dunkk knew he couldn't do it. It had to be someone whom had a strong bond with Eddie and had been untouched by Shark Waters.

"I got a plan that just might work, Major."

"I'm all ears, Slamm," Ursa Majoris said attentively.

And Slamm Dunkk told him.

"We have to hit the ground running," Slamm Dunkk said after he revealed his strategy to Ursa Majoris. "Once we get out of here, we go our separate ways. I'll do what I have to do, and you'll contact the other Spirits and you guys will do your thing."

Ursa Majoris said, "Got it."

"So, we ready?"

"Let's do it!" Ursa Majoris said as the two of them crisscrossed their arms and held each other's wrists.

"We have to do it with total concentration," Slamm Dunkk barked, huddling close to Ursa Majoris.

Both of them closed their eyes and chanted under their breaths with the utmost concentration. The entire chamber began to rumble, and out of nowhere, high above the chamber, blue and yellow lightning bolts flashed, brightening it up like the obnoxious and over-the-top neon signs of the main Las Vegas strip. The Spirits' chants grew louder and louder until a brown-orange sphere surrounded the two of them and muffled their chants.

Carrying the Spirits, the sphere slowly rose up toward the ceiling where the bolts were wickedly flashing and exploding in the air; two bolts, one blue and the other yellow, zeroed in on the sphere and collided into it intentionally, creating a long, blinding white flash that permeated throughout the whole chamber. And the moment the objects impacted, there was a thunderous roar that seemed to reverberate forever in the chamber.

And then, suddenly, akin to the feeling after a huge earthquake, there was absolute silence and stillness. Both Slamm Dunk and Ursa Majoris were nowhere in sight. They were free.

"Eddie! Eddie! Eddie!"

The crowd's chant grew so loud, Eddie was sure that it could be heard for miles. Poised to sign the contract in front of the mass of people, he studied them just below him. His family and friends—all of them who were previously against him pursuing his dreams—were in now full support of him, egging him on to sign that oh-so-important document.

Eddie took a deep breath. It was indeed a magic moment, and he wanted to savor every second of it. He glanced at Shark Waters, who seemed at his fattest—just how many pounds had he put on in the last two days—and Waters handed him a gold pen. Slowly, Eddie removed the cap of the pen and looked down at the contract on the podium.

I can't believe this is happening.

As he put the pen to the paper, someone screamed out, "Don't sign it, Eddie!"

Then another but younger voice followed, "Yeah, Eddie, don't do it!"

There was one huge collective gasp from the crowd, and Eddie looked up immediately and examined every face in the courtyard. And there they were.

The party crashers. The uninvited guests who wanted to spoil it for everyone: Richie Sykes and Aaron Holder.

Aaron?

Eddie was astounded and speechless at the sight of his younger brother, who was clutching onto Richie's hand so tightly. He simply couldn't understand why and how Aaron was here. He so dearly wanted Aaron to be at this party, but not this way. It was the ultimate betrayal to come here with Richie.

"Don't do it!" Richie yelled even louder.

Pulling Aaron along, Richie pushed his way through the astonished crowd with the unexpected visit by that Spirit, Aquila, still stirring vividly in his memory. It was altogether a bizarre and haunting experience, but Richie clearly understood why Eddie was acting the way he was. And now, as nerve-wracking as it was, it fell to him as well as Aaron to save Eddie from ruin, and they would do it, no matter what the costs.

"Get them out of here!" Waters barked.

Richie and Aaron were climbing up the stage, and they both stared pleadingly at Eddie.

Aaron screamed out, "Please don't do this, Eddie. If you do this, I know I'll never see you again!"

A couple of beefy security guards grabbed the two from behind and began pulling them away. Aaron cried out in surprise, while Richie struggled, but he was no match for the guards.

In a panic, Richie bellowed, "You'll ruin your life. Waters is a fraud. He's going to ruin your life! Please, Eddie, don't do it! You're making the biggest mistake of your life!"

"Shut him up!"

As the guards pulled him away from the platform, Richie cried, "Eddie, you can't even beat me now. What makes you think you'll measure up to the pros?"

Eddie just stood without movement, watching Richie and Aaron being hauled away. His head felt like it was going to explode. One moment, he was on top of the world, and the next moment, it felt like he was falling from it.

"Waters doesn't want to help you. He's evil! He has everybody believing that you're 'it'! But it's all a lie."

Eddie screamed at the top of his lungs. Images of the past and present exploded and collided through his mind, and he fell to the ground, clutching his throbbing head with both of his hands tightly.

"Nooooo! What am I supposed to do?"

"Holder, sign that contract!" Shark commanded frantically. "Do it now before it's too late!"

Trying to fight through the pain, Eddie stole a look at Waters, who was approaching him with intense ferocity. But that was the last thing that seemed concrete to him. Everything before him—even his own body—seemed to melt away into a hazy white…

CHAPTER 12

The Spirit of Basketball Future

"Edward Holder...Edward Holder, wake up." The voice seemed so close but yet so far.

Slowly, Eddie opened his eyes and saw Slamm Dunkk sitting next to him on a bed. Eddie knew right away where he was: his bedroom.

His headache was gone, but now, Eddie felt a certain apprehension about what was going to happen next.

"Edward, there's one more thing that I have to show you," Slamm Dunkk said.

"I don't have much of a choice, do I?" Eddie said weakly.

"Sorry, Edward."

Eddie knew what was next. Slamm Dunkk would chant some kind of spell or snap his fingers, and Eddie would be whisked away to some unknown place. He tried to mentally prepare himself quickly for the journey to another dimension, but this time, much to his relief and surprise, it was the bedroom that changed to pitch black.

Eddie squinted his eyes to try and make shapes out in the dark, and, as he did so, there was a quick, bright flash. The blackness around him changed instantaneously, and Eddie was now in a small, dark windowless room with one bed, a chair in one corner and nothing else. A single bulb hung from the ceiling, the paint on the walls was chipping away, and the carpet was quite bare and worn out. Eddie sensed the cold and loneliness of the room, but at the same time, the atmosphere of the room seemed a bit staged, not quite real. Eddie felt like he was in an audience watching a dramatic play.

In the one chair sat a lone figure staring blankly at the one poster that adorned the room. The poster was of a younger Michael Jordan stretching his arms out to the side.

"Welcome to the future of Eddie Holder," Slamm Dunkk announced.

"Where are we?" Eddie asked. "Is that me sitting in that chair?"

"Yes, it's about two years from the present," Slamm Dunkk answered sadly.

There was a knock on the door. Dressed in tattered jeans and a faded blue t-shirt, Eddie Holder got off the chair and answered the door. He looked old and tired and lacked the energy and enthusiasm that the younger Eddie Holder had.

"Yes?" Eddie said.

A hunchbacked old man who had cold and mean eyes stood at the doorway. He spoke in a thick European accent, "Where is this month's rent? You are already a week late."

Shaking his head, Eddie shrugged. "I need a couple of more days."

"How many times do you do this to me? I have given you so many chances," the old man grunted. "You give me the rent in the next couple of days, and then you find another place to live. I have no choice."

"But, Mr. Barone…"

"No more chances. I'm tired of you. Good day." Mr. Barone turned and stomped away.

"Well, good day to you, too," Eddie muttered under his breath, closing the door.

Eddie walked to the bed and plopped down on it. Sighing deeply, he closed his eyes, remembering happier times in his life. Before Eddie and Slamm Dunkk, the entire room grew dim and dissolved into the El Camino Park basketball courts where a younger Eddie was sitting and joking around with Sam, Flash and Richie. Then El Camino Park dissolved into the living room of the Holder household where Eddie, Aaron and Dad sat happily, watching a basketball game on television. The setting again shifted, this time into a classroom with Miss Lane talking to Eddie, who had a big smile on his face. Then the classroom scene dimmed and transformed back into the lonely apartment room of Eddie.

Sighing again, Eddie got up and pulled out a shoebox from under the bed. Inside the shoebox was a stack of folded letters. He took out one of the letters from the top and carefully unfolded it. Enclosed with the letter was an ATM card. He read the letter as he clutched the card tightly, holding it close to his heart.

"Oh, Mom," Eddie said quietly to himself as tears started rolling down his cheeks.

Eddie closed his eyes and reminisced about the events leading to his coming to Europe. The room darkened yet once again and changed into the entrance area of the Holder home.

By the door was one suitcase, and standing next to the suitcase was Eddie arguing with his dad and mom. Dad had a grim look on his face, while Mom was dabbing her wet eyes with a blue handkerchief. Aaron was holding Mom's hand as he wept hysterically.

"You can't do this, Eddie," Dad asked. "How are you going to support yourself?"

"This ain't none of your concern no more," Eddie said coldly. "I made my decision already."

"We're your parents, Eddie. You can't shut us out like this," Mom sobbed.

Eddie shrugged coldly.

"Eddie, don't do this!" Dad grabbed Eddie's arm, desperate to keep his son from going.

Eddie demanded loudly, "Let go of me, old man!"

"Don't do this," Dad said again. "You're making a big mistake. Let's talk about it."

"You mean, talk about how you want to control my life and screw it up for me forever?" Eddie growled. "Now, let go of me!"

"If you take a foot out this door, don't ever expect to come back!" Dad meant every word of it.

"Just get outta my way!" Eddie hollered.

Suddenly, Eddie slapped his dad's hand away and shoved him away with much force. Dad stumbled backward, knocking over the suitcase and falling to the ground. He gaped at Eddie in utter shock.

"How could you?" Dad asked.

Without looking at his dad, Eddie grabbed the suitcase that had fallen on its side and exited the house. He walked down the walkway as quickly as he could to Waters' 350Z parked at the curb.

From the house, he heard his dad bellow out, "Let him go, Rachel."

"I can't," Mom yelled back, rushing out of the house as she pulled Aaron along.

Eddie got into the car and started the engine. He was about to pull away from the curb when his mom and Aaron jumped in front of the car, preventing him from moving forward. Eddie put the car into park and looked at both his mom and Aaron cheerlessly.

Aaron screamed out, "Big brother, don't go!"

Eddie looked down with deep felt guilt. He hated disappointing the little man, but he had his life.

"Eddie, take this," Mom cried, grabbing Eddie's left hand from the steering wheel and putting a card in it. "Use it. Your father doesn't have to know."

"Look, I really have to go," Eddie said weakly. "Take care, mom. And you, too, Aaron."

Neither Mom nor Aaron could respond as tears rolled down both of their cheeks.

Eddie drove off, and as he looked in the rearview mirror, he saw his mom sink to her knees and bury her face in her hands. Aaron clung to her tightly like glue.

"Nice going, hot-shot," Slamm Dunkk said suddenly.

Eddie turned to Slamm Dunkk. "But, I didn't…"

"You will if you continue on like this," Slamm Dunkk said sternly. "You want to do this to your folks?"

"No," Eddie whispered as he looked down sadly. He had never seen his mom like this before, and the last thing he wanted was to make her suffer. And he definitely didn't want to hurt Aaron. Was it actually going to happen this way? Surely, there was a way to prevent this tragic event from happening.

"Let's move on," Slamm Dunkk said.

Eddie looked up and saw that the street scene had switched magically to a locker room setting. The locker room was full of players changing into their uniforms as they spoke to each other excitedly. There was a lot of camaraderie among the players, but away from it all, in one far corner, sat an older Eddie Holder in front of his locker. He was with Shark Waters, who was dressed in a fashionable dark gray European suit, smoking a stogie.

"So, what can I do for you, Eddie?" Shark said calmly, taking a puff from his cigar.

"You mind putting that out?" Eddie requested.

"Of course, I do. It's Cuban," Shark said. "We can't get Cuban in America."

"I don't care about your freakin' cigar!" Eddie said forcefully.

Shark arched an eyebrow. "Oh?"

"I'm getting kicked out of the apartment. I need money now. It's bad enough that I can barely make ends meet." Eddie's voice was weak.

Shark Waters shrugged his shoulders. "Not my fault."

"Yes, it is," Eddie accused. "It's been over two years, and I'm still stuck in this European developmental league."

Eddie was so angry he could barely get the words out, but he continued on, "All those things you promised me didn't come true. I haven't become professional. You didn't get me into no mentoring program. I ain't got a high school diploma, and I've been playing for this crappy European league in these crappy arenas for the last two friggin' years!"

"What do you want me to say, Eddie?" Shark said coolly, taking another puff of his cigar. "You know, the deal was twenty-five thousand US American dollars, and you only paid me about ten grand, but I let you slide on the rest, because when we signed up for this league, you said it was okay for me to get half of your salary. But, honestly, this league doesn't pay squat, and I'm still out my fees, my airfares, let alone, other expenditures that you owe me. No, I'm afraid the question is not what can Herbert Waters do for Eddie Holder, but what can Eddie Holder do for Herbert Waters. How is Eddie Holder going to pay back Herbert Waters all the money that he owes him?"

"Don't give me none of that, you and your fancy suits and Cuban cigars," Eddie said.

"Oh, big talk from a kid who can't pay his bills!" Shark shook his head. "You owe me, buddy, you owe me big time for all the favors I've done for you. You're lucky that I still answer your phone calls. If I weren't such a softie, I would drop you."

Shark took a long puff on his Cuban stogie and then continued, "Oh, Edward, you gave me such high hopes. I invested so much time and energy in you, but you turned out to be nothing but a disappointment. You don't have enough talent to make it even here in Europe. Then again, if you paid me the rest of the money, we wouldn't be having this conversation."

"So, if I don't pay you, then I'm stuck here forever in this league."

"That's right," Shark said. "No money, no honey. But, then again, two years ago, the rate was twenty-five. Now, it's up to forty plus the fees that you owe me. How do you expect to come up with that sort of money?"

Eddie stood up and slammed his fist into his locker. His knuckles started bleeding, and the sting was quite sharp, but Eddie did not show any pain in front of Shark Waters.

"I want out," Eddie said. "You hear me? I want out."

Shark pointed rudely at Eddie with his cigar. "You signed a contract with the league, and if you leave right now, you'll be in breach. Certainly, you don't want that."

Eddie rubbed his bloody knuckles. "No, but you need to get me out somehow."

Shark smiled a ruthless smile. "Eddie, don't call me anymore with your sorry old problems that you claim is my fault. Call me when you have the money to pay me back. Until then, I want nothing to do with you."

With the cigar, Shark saluted and walked away from Eddie.

"So, this is your future," Slamm Dunkk announced. "How sad…"

Eddie couldn't say a word as he watched his older self slink down in defeat onto the bench in front of his locker. Then he looked at Slamm Dunkk with an expression of doubt.

"What can I do, Slamm Dunkk?" he asked.

"I think you know the answer to that," Slamm Dunkk replied. "There is more to come."

The locker room scenery had changed into a basketball arena, and both Eddie and Slamm Dunkk were sitting courtside at a basketball game already in progress. With more than half of the seats empty, the arena was not state-of-the art like the current basketball centers in America. In fact, it resembled a high school gymnasium; old fashioned, dilapidated and dirty with stale popcorn, peanut shells, cigarette butts, newspapers, and old basketball programs scattered about everywhere on the ground.

"What is this place?" Eddie said.

"We're here at one of your games. Oh, yes, there you are."

Slamm Dunkk pointed toward an older Eddie Holder dribbling the ball near half court. The present Eddie watched intently, and he couldn't help but sense a feeling of *déjà vu*. The future Eddie faked to his right and then went immediately to the left to blow pass his defender in front of him. And although one of his teammates broke free for a wide-open shot, Eddie drove to the basket rather than pass the ball.

"Pass the ball," the younger Eddie shouted.

But Eddie chose to take an ill-advised shot. Out of control and nowhere to advance because the defense was tight, Eddie weakly finger-rolled the ball toward the hoop. The shot was short; it clanged off the rim, and the opposing center grabbed the rebound with authority. Quickly, he threw a pass down the court to his open teammate, and the teammate flipped the ball up and in, making an easy lay-up.

Eddie's team was now down twenty-five points, and the small crowd began to boo loudly, some taunting Eddie for his play and others screaming for him to go back home to America.

"Old habits die hard," Slamm Dunkk remarked.

The present Eddie Holder didn't say a word because he couldn't agree more.

The rest of the game was basically a runaway. The other team was up by almost thirty points. Eddie's team lacked the fight and energy to mount a comeback. But who could blame anyone of them? Every time Eddie Holder got the ball in his hands—which was more than half of the time—he drove to the basket out of control, not willing to pass the ball to any of his teammates, and more often than not, he forced incredible shots that had no chance of going in whatsoever. The Beatles had a better chance of making a comeback tour.

Although the coach had begged Eddie to get his teammates involved during the timeouts, it didn't work. Benching him for long periods of time didn't help, either. It just made Eddie all the more determined to shine. But the future Eddie Holder just didn't get it. By trying to show off his fancy moves and his individual skills only made the crowd turn on him and basketball scouts sour on him. *Eddie Holder doesn't have what it takes to go pro…he's too selfish…he doesn't care about winning…he just wants individual glory.*

As the younger Eddie watched the game, he grew visibly upset and whined, "Can we leave now? I get the picture."

"We'll stay a little longer," Slamm Dunkk said. "It won't kill you to watch a bit more."

Pleading his case, Eddie said, "Look, I said I get it already. Please, can we just go?"

"Just watch the game, my boy." Slamm Dunkk knew it was killing Eddie inside, but he had to push the envelope.

Eddie shrugged and turned his attention back to the basketball game. There were a couple of minutes left in the game, and the future Eddie Holder was back on the floor, playing defense now.

The player that Eddie was guarding was a bit taller, and he had his body in a slight crouch. With the left side of his body fronting Eddie, he dribbled the ball skillfully with his right hand. Eddie watched his opponent's torso with full concentration, and when the player swiveled to his left, Eddie saw his opening. He outstretched his right arm, poking the ball away from the opposing player. And the ball squirted away.

There was a mad scramble. Eddie dove for the ball, his body making solid contact with the hardwood floor, and as he barely got his right hand on the ball, the opposing player who was also in pursuit accidentally tripped over Eddie's arm and stumbled to the ground.

Immediately, Eddie felt a sharp pain shooting up his right arm, but still he scooped up the ball with his left hand and dribbled down the court as quickly as he could. There was clear access to the basket, and, as he jumped to do a left-handed windmill jam, out of nowhere, another defender swooped in and slammed forcefully into Eddie in mid-air.

Eddie landed awkwardly on the side of one foot, his knee crumpling under him and his forward momentum taking him into the seats behind the back-board. Eddie banged the top of his head on one of the metal chairs. The sound of his skull hitting metal made an extremely horrifying snapping sound loud enough to echo throughout the entire arena, and Eddie lay still atop of the chairs that had turned over. A hush lay over the arena, and only the quiet hum of the old air conditioner was audible.

The pain was all too real for the present Eddie Holder, and he clearly got the message. There was a nauseating feeling in the pit of his stomach. "Can we please go now?"

Nodding his head, Slamm Dunkk said, "As you wish."

Slamm Dunkk raised his arms back and forth, chanting quietly. The entire arena setting blurred into a sort of white fuzziness. After a moment or so, another scenery came into focus, replacing the arena. Eddie and Slamm Dunkk were now looking at a quiet hospital room.

The room was big and private; the future Eddie Holder sat up in the bed. His left leg was elevated in a cast, while his bandaged right arm lay flat by his side. Eddie stared blankly at the rain that was falling hard and steady outside. The gloomy rainy day fit his mood perfectly.

The door to the room creaked open and Eddie turned to see who it was. It was Shark Waters, who was talking on his cell phone as usual. Eddie made a lit-tle sigh and turned back to look out the window at the rain.

"I'll talk to you later. Remember, my man, you are my shining star!" Waters said as sweetly as honey and then turned the phone off.

"Another one of your suckas?" Eddie asked sarcastically, still staring out the window.

"I didn't come here to get insulted by the likes of you," Shark snarled, immediately becoming cold and distant.

"So, what do you want?" Eddie asked, finally turning to look at Shark with hatred.

Shark sat in the chair next to the bed, crossing his legs. He was dressed in another fancy European suit, but it didn't fit him well. The buttoned jacket was snug around the waist, and with his legs crossed, the fabric of the pants pulled quite a bit, making it quite tight around his thighs. It was obvious to Eddie Holder that despite the constant cry for money, Shark Waters was living the good life, eating well, partying hard and gaining more weight than ever.

Shark said flatly, "I just spoke with the league office, and with your injuries and all, they decided to terminate your contract. Of course, they'll pay all medical expenses. You'll get a minimal severance pay, which they will pay to me directly."

"I want all of that severance pay. I need the money."

"Is that concussion of yours worse than it is?" Shark let out an ugly snort. "You owe me money and I'm taking it all."

"I need the money to get back home and start over again."

Shark remarked mockingly, "Hopefully, not in basketball."

Eddie let the comment slide.

Shark continued, "I've gone beyond the call of duty, but hey, since I'm such a sweetheart of a guy, I'll give you fifteen percent of the severance pay. That should pay for your flight back and then some."

Eddie just stared at Shark. The room was silent except for the steady fall of the rain. Somewhere out in the distance, there was a low rumbling sound and then a flash of light outside the window.

"Fine," Eddie said finally. "What about my parents? Did you contact them?"

Shark shook his head emphatically.

"Did you even try?" Eddie asked suspiciously.

"Of course, I did," Shark yelled back. "They weren't at the number you gave me. I tried a couple of times, but nada. Zilch. Nothing."

Frustrated, Eddie turned away from Shark to look out the window again. He could feel the tears well up in his eyes and rubbed them. If anything, he wasn't going to give Shark Waters the satisfaction of seeing him cry.

"Eddie," Shark said. "There's still the issue of money."

Not wanting to look at the greedy pig's face, Eddie continued to look out the window.

"How are you going to pay me back?" Shark persisted.

Without answering, Eddie just shook his head, staring out at the pouring rain.

"Answer me, Eddie!" Shark stood up with dramatic flair. "You've been in this hospital for a couple of weeks with all this time on your hands to think, but you still have no clue about how you're going to pay me back. You disappoint me."

"Too bad," Eddie growled. "I don't know what planet you're from, but you ain't even on my radar."

Eddie's voice grew louder. "And even if you planned to sue me, go ahead. I ain't got nothing at all. Send your lawyers after me! Send the cops after me! I just don't friggin' care no more."

"Everything is gone, Waters!" Eddie was now hollering at the top of his lungs. "My family...the education you promised me...the basketball career you promised me...the fame you promised me! All of it, gone! The only thing I have left is a messed up knee that's torn to shreds and nerve damage in both the right arm and right leg. So if you wanna come after me, go ahead. I got nothing to give you!"

Unable to say a word, Shark glared at Eddie for a long moment and then stalked out of the room, slamming the door hard.

Eddie Holder was truly alone now. He sat quietly listening to the pounding rain. Then, in a desperate measure, Eddie suddenly grabbed the phone on the counter next to his bed and dialed a number he had not called in a long time, but he still remembered the number by heart. It was the number he called wherever he needed a ride home from school; it was the number that he called whenever he was going to have dinner at a friend's house; it was the number he could always depend on—it was home.

Eddie believed that Shark tried to contact his parents, but he had to be certain. There was a long pause and then some static on the other end. And then the phone began to ring. Eddie's heart thumped rapidly in anticipation of hearing his mom or his dad answer the phone. His palms felt clammy as he gripped the phone tightly with his left hand.

It rang once, twice and a third time. Then there was a click. Somebody was picking up the phone.

"Hello," Eddie shouted with joy.

"The number you have reached is no longer in service. If you feel..."

Eddie dropped the receiver in his lap in shock.

"What's going on? Where's my family?" the present Eddie asked as if he were vocalizing the future Eddie's thoughts.

"Apparently moved away," Slamm Dunkk said quickly.

"But why didn't they let me know or something?" Eddie murmured weakly. "At least, my mom could have."

"Perhaps," Slamm Dunkk said, nodding his head slightly. "But remember all those letters you saw in that shoebox?"

Eddie thought about it for a moment. "Yeah."

Slamm Dunkk explained dryly, "All those letters were from your mother and Aaron that went unanswered. Not a one, and it's been—what—more than two years? It's a wonder that your mother and little brother continued to write all that time even though you never wrote back."

At a loss for words, Eddie examined his future self who sat miserably alone on the bed. It was hard for Eddie to not feel sorry for his future self, but deep down inside, Eddie knew this depressing so-called future was his own doing.

"We're almost at the end here," Slamm Dunkk announced. "It's time to witness just a couple of more things."

Shrugging his shoulders, Eddie said without any resistance, "Sure, whatever you say."

The hospital room dimmed to black, and the setting that came into focus before Eddie was roughly ten years into the future. With the overall tone seemingly cold, grim and gray, the glimpse of this particular future did not offer a kind or promising picture.

The future Eddie Holder was now frail, very old looking and dressed shabbily, despite only being in his late twenties. He walked with a noticeable and painful limp, using an old beat-up cane. And as the present Eddie Holder watched, it became apparent to him that the future Eddie Holder was back in the old neighborhood, searching for a job. Going from door to door, the future Eddie Holder met with potential employers of grocery stores, drug stores, gas stations and the like, but each and every time, he was turned away because no one wanted to hire a high-school dropout who was physically challenged, both in his legs and hands.

It was grueling for the present Eddie to watch all of his future struggles. But what hit him the hardest was when the setting had changed to the former Holder household. The house was obviously abandoned and had a depressing feeling. And because it was pouring rain at the moment, the sad, lonely feeling was all the more suffocating. The front lawn that was once so green and watered and mowed with tender loving care by his dad had turned into a hideous patch of brown, and the shrubs and bushes that were trimmed neatly every month without fail had become gnarled and grew wildly, as if they belonged to a wicked witch's residence.

The once smooth walkway was marred with ugly cracks and scuffmarks, while the windows of the house were smeared with brown dirt and the gooey residue of dead bugs that had smashed against them. The four small stained glass windows of the door had been shattered, and the door itself had been tagged with graffiti claiming the end of the world. So much for the neighborhood watch program…

This abandoned house was no longer the home that Eddie knew. It was no longer the house that was once colorful, joyful and bustling with life, and Eddie's heart ached so much it felt like it was about to explode. His heart hurt all the more when he saw the future Eddie Holder stumbling up the walkway and getting drenched from the unforgiving rain.

The future Eddie Holder called out for his dad, mom and little brother, hoping that someone would come out to greet him. He stared at the front door, but unfortunately, the door did not open, and Eddie sat glumly on the front porch and wept intensely.

The present Eddie Holder sighed deeply.

"Final chapter!" Slamm Dunkk's voice was loud and startled Eddie a bit.

The former Holder household setting was now the front of a neighborhood grocery store with a small parking lot in front. It was a cold winter evening, and the storefront was decorated with Christmas lights and signs that read, *Joy to the World* or *We Wish You a Merry Christmas*. The ground was wet from the recent rain, and the blacktop had a certain wet gleam to it. Coming out of the store with the collars of their jackets up, customers rushed home with plans of warming themselves up with hot coffee or eggnog in the comforts of their own homes.

A metallic gray SUV pulled into a parking slot near the entrance of the store. There was a couple in the SUV, and they got out and walked toward the entrance of the store holding hands.

"They seem familiar," Eddie said quietly.

"Look carefully," Slamm Dunkk said.

Eddie studied the features of the couple intently. Then he realized it was Richie and Alicia, but they were much older. Eddie couldn't help but notice the wedding rings on both of their fingers, and immediately, Eddie felt a tinge of jealousy and envy.

"It's going to be great getting together with Flash and Sam tonight. It's been a long time," Richie said with enthusiasm.

"How long has it been?" Alicia asked as she leaned her head against Richie's arm.

"Geez, I don't know. The last time I saw Flash was when he was just starting law school at Harvard. And that was almost two years ago."

Alicia laughed. "Who would have thought? A loud-mouthed, flashy high school point guard turning into a loud-mouthed flashy hotshot lawyer with a Japanese accent. I guess it's still the same."

As Richie held the store door open, he chuckled, "So true, but I'm so glad that he's decided to move his practice back here now. I missed him."

Eddie asked, "So, what does Richie do?"

Slamm Dunkk watched Richie and Alicia shop through the window glass. "Oh, he's a movie director. Pretty much in demand and extremely successful. On the weekends, he coaches a boys' basketball league. They like him a lot."

Eddie nodded to himself as if he was proud of Richie. "So, what about Alicia?"

Slamm Dunkk answered, "Alicia's a college professor, but right now, she's just about three months pregnant although she doesn't know it."

"They mentioned Sam. What does he do in the future?"

"He's in sports medicine, and on his spare time, he gives Richie a hand with the team on the weekends."

Finally, Richie and Alicia came out of the store with three bags full of groceries and walked to their SUV. Alicia went inside the SUV, while Richie loaded the groceries into the back.

As Richie loaded the car, a man wearing tattered clothes and a grimy baseball cap staggered up to him and put out his hand. He was homeless and had a rank stench to him. It was obvious the homeless person had not bathed for days, maybe months.

"Please, sir, can you spare some change?" the homeless person asked in a gravelly voice.

Richie studied the homeless man. "I don't have any change, but here's a bag of potato chips and a ham sandwich."

The homeless guy snatched the bag of chips and the sandwich and limped away as quickly as he could.

"You're welcome," Richie hollered to the homeless guy. "And Merry Christmas to you."

The homeless guy didn't react and sat down at the curbside of the grocery store under the shadows of a streetlight. Shrugging his shoulders, Richie entered the SUV and left the parking lot.

It had begun to rain lightly, and the streetlights illuminated the falling rain-drops vividly. Sadly, Eddie watched the homeless man devour the sandwich and potato chips eagerly. The food was gone in a matter of seconds, and the homeless man sat on the ground, shaking and mumbling to himself. He looked pathetic and lonely. Eddie felt extremely sorry for the man.

The rain began to fall harder, and the homeless man gazed up into the dark, gray sky. And as if there was some sense of urgency, the homeless man stood up at attention and went to the spotlight of the streetlamp. For no reason at all, he began to spin, doing a little jig and peeling off his filthy jacket. Faster and faster, he spun, until all at once he crumpled down into an exhausted heap. Then, all of a sudden, the homeless man began to laugh without rhyme or rea-son. Angrily, he tore off his baseball cap and turned to look directly at Eddie.

In the homeless man's eyes, there was hatred, rage and madness, and for the first time, Eddie saw his face clearly and was sickened to his stomach. The homeless man was Eddie Holder!

"It can't be. It just can't be..." Eddie whined to himself. "Why did this have to happen?"

"It's time to go now," Slamm Dunkk said coldly as he grabbed Eddie's arm.

"Noooo...Noooo..."

"It just can't be!"

Eddie yelled at the top of his lungs and then realized that he was no longer with Slamm Dunkk. Nor was he in the future. He was back at the party, crouched down with his hands clutching his head. But he felt like himself again. He felt reborn, complete and strong.

"Sign that contract, Holder!" Shark bellowed out murderously.

Eddie stood up immediately and grabbed the pen off the podium. He peeked at the crowd, and everyone was standing still like zombies. Then he looked quickly at Richie and Aaron, who were still struggling with the guards. Richie shook his head heatedly, pleading with Eddie not to sign the contract.

"No, Eddie, please don't!" Aaron cried out, thinking that all was hopeless.

Smiling widely, Eddie winked at both Richie and Aaron to show that he had it all under control.

"Now, Holder!"

How could I have been so blind? This dude's getting on my last nerve!

Eddie scribbled something down on the contract, and then he handed it to Shark politely. Shark grabbed it, looked at the signature immediately and dropped the contract to the ground as if it were on fire.

"What is the meaning of this, Holder?" Shark growled, feeling a bit weak in the knees.

Eddie spread out his arms wide and deadpanned, "Hey, you said you wanted my John Hancock, so I gave it to you."

"And another thing," Eddie continued, feeling stronger every minute. "Here's your money back. Use it to lose some of that disgusting weight, Herbert."

Reaching into his inside coat pocket, Eddie pulled out a long envelope and tossed it on the ground. In horror, Waters gawked at the envelope containing the money. Beads of perspiration formed on his upper lip, and then, all at once, his whole body began to contract and expand violently as if he were hooked up to a helium tank and someone was playing with the gauge.

"No!" Herbert screamed.

Now, Shark began to wobble around the stage uncontrollably, and it was getting harder and harder for him to breathe. Like a fish on the verge of death, he opened his mouth to suck in some air, but instead of breathing in air, Shark vomited! Hundreds upon hundreds of white semi-transparent phantom-like objects with vague human heads burst from his mouth and floated up to the night sky. Waters covered his mouth, but the phantom-like objects continued to pour forth, and there wasn't a thing Waters could do. He was losing all the souls that he had absorbed.

Eddie couldn't believe what he was happening. Right before his very eyes, Shark was losing weight at a miraculous rate, while the phantom-like objects spewed forth from his mouth. And as the phantom-like objects reached toward the sky, everyone in the crowd, except for Richie and Aaron, began to vanish into thin air one by one.

"Let's get outta here!" Eddie shouted out to Richie and Aaron.

Eddie jumped off the stage and scooped up his little brother. He nodded at Richie, and the two began to run off as fast as they could toward the archway that served as an exit. But as the two made their escape, the entire area began to quake powerfully and the ground beneath them was torn apart. Huge fissures the size of Grand Canyon started opening up all around them, gobbling up the archway first, and then the magnificent ice sculptures and palm trees, and finally, the rows of tables in a hurry.

"This way's no good!" Eddie screamed above the tremor. "We gotta head back."

Eddie made a quick U-turn, and, as he ran, still holding onto Aaron for dear life, he scanned the stage to see if there was a way out. The stage was now devoid of people—Shark Waters had apparently made a hasty retreat—and unfortunately, there seemed to be no exit at first glance. But Eddie looked a little harder, and there it was. A tiny hole in a concrete wall to the right of the stage. He didn't know where it led to, but they had to take a chance.

"Over there," Eddie hollered at the same time the ground beneath them began to rumble again.

Aaron screamed out in terror.

"It's okay, little bro, we'll get outta here," Eddie said as soothingly as possible although he wasn't so sure.

"Eddie!" Richie shouted out from behind.

Eddie looked back to see that another fissure had opened up directly behind them and was quickly gaining on them. Eddie made a mad dash for the opening, followed closely by Richie, but Richie tripped over something in his path and fell to his knees.

"Eddie!"

Eddie turned around and went back to help Richie up, but the area immediately underneath Eddie opened up like the mouth of a hungry tiger and swallowed them up. The three of them plummeted into a deep, dark hole, screaming their heads off. It looked like the end for them all…

…but, miraculously an orange-brown sphere appeared out of nowhere and enveloped the three of them. They had been saved!

Aaron, who was thoroughly spooked about the whole thing, asked his older brother, "What's going on, Eddie?"

Eddie held onto his brother tightly. "We're okay, Aaron. We're okay."

The sphere floated up out of the hole and flew up to the sky. Eddie looked through the sphere and saw Ursa Majoris guiding the sphere with his mystical powers through the night sky.

Eddie looked at Richie, and he gave him a nod and a smile. Richie smiled back, and all at once, all three of the boys looked down and marveled at the beautiful, twinkling city that knew nothing of the horrible trouble they had just experienced. But, it didn't matter. The nightmare was over.

Eddie pulled Aaron closer to him, and he felt the warmth of his brother's body. It was a good feeling. No, it was a great feeling. Cradling his brother tightly, Eddie closed his eyes and fell into a deep, comfortable sleep…

Heading toward the beach down below, a weak Shark Waters slid down the rocky hill behind the house frantically. He had Eddie, but everything just went haywire without any rhyme or reason. To see it unravel right before his very eyes was simply unbelievable and unacceptable. He had calculated everything, and yet it "hit the fan" so quickly. Eddie had turned against him in a blink of an eye and that was the end of it all. How could it all go so wrong?

Finally, Shark reached the base of the hill and sat down on the cool sand, huffing and puffing. He may have lost the battle today, but he knew there would be other naïve Eddie Holders of the world, who were chomping at the bit to become professional athletes. He would have to re-energize himself and rise up strong again.

"Boy, you go on a crash diet or what?" a voice asked behind him.

Shark looked back up toward the hill and saw Slamm Dunkk sitting just above him on the slope of the hill.

Shark stood up angrily. "You? How?"

"What happened? All that weight loss cause brain damage or something?" Slamm Dunkk grinned widely at Shark. "Did you honestly think you were going to get away with this? You didn't bank on Eddie being so strong and pure, did you?"

Slamm Dunkk snapped his fingers and disappeared. When he reappeared, he was standing directly in front of Shark. Only this time he wasn't alone. Standing beside him were Perseus, Pegasus, Aquila and Orion. All of them had on their "game faces."

"Big blunder, buddy." Slamm Dunkk poked Shark in the chest hard. "And you didn't even bank on me getting out of the Ghetto. Hey, don't underestimate the power of good! Ever!"

Shark couldn't say a word. He turned to escape, but Aquila moved to block his path.

"Oh, yeah, and one more thing," Slamm Dunkk said, "Sharkie, my boy, remember how I said I'll banish you to another dimension and you laughed in my face?"

Slamm Dunkk had a very smug look on his face as he pulled a two-page document from out of nowhere. He shoved it in front of Shark's face, and, in turn, Shark hastily grabbed it and began to read it.

"Well, guess what?" Slamm Dunkk gave Shark a big, big smile.

As Shark skimmed through the document, horror registered on his gaunt face.

"You have been served. Bye-bye!" Slamm Dunkk waved at Shark Waters.

"No, this can't be happening!" Shark Waters lunged at Slamm Dunkk, but the other Spirits charged in front to protect Slamm Dunkk.

"Yes, I'm afraid this is happening."

Slamm Dunkk snapped his fingers, and then a shaft of light came down from the sky and enveloped Shark Waters. The moment the beam of light enclosed Shark, he felt the intense heat and globs of perspiration dripping down his face immediately. He tried to escape, but when he took a step, his foot felt like mush. Shark Water's body was melting like butter in a hot skillet.

"Nooooooo!"

Shark screamed out as his legs and then his body turned into a puddle of goop. Shark struggled like a man sinking in quicksand, reaching for something to pull himself out from the dreadful fate that awaited him. Shark tried to shout out something—anything—but it was too late. His whole evil essence vanished, exiled to another dimension. And the only thing left of Shark Waters was his pink tuxedo and toupee in a heap.

"Sorry, old chap," Slamm Dunkk said, grabbing the toupee and twirling it with his finger mischievously. "The case has come to a sizzling finish."

Eddie jolted up from his bed drenched in sweat. He looked around his surroundings with a feeling of dread, panic and confusion; and when he finally realized that he was back in the confines of his bedroom, he gave a deep sigh of relief. The nightmare was indeed over.

Eddie sat quietly on the bed for a moment. Tears welled up in his eyes, and they streaked down his cheek. They were tears of joy. Tears of relief. He was a changed person. It had been a long journey, but the old Eddie Holder was back, and somehow or another he knew that he had to make it up to his family and his friends.

The road to fully regaining everyone's friendship and trust would be a long and winding one. However, gaining what he had lost academically would be even tougher. His task was cut out for him, and Eddie was quite aware that he could not waste any more time, not even for a second.

He got up and went to the bedroom window, pulling up the shades. As he looked out, he touched his ear. The big gaudy gold earring on his left ear was gone, and even the 350Z was no longer parked by the curbside where he had left it this morning. There were no more remnants of Shark Waters.

Smiling to himself, Eddie then sat at his desk and cracked opened a notebook. And it felt good.

CHAPTER 13

Wrapping Up Loose Ends

It was Sunday morning. The family was having brunch in the dining room when Eddie came trudging in with his hands behind his back. He looked a bit sleepy, but he had a smile on his face that was full of sunshine.

"Good morning!" Eddie shouted with glee.

"Good morning," Mom greeted without emotion.

"Hi, Eddie!" Aaron gave his brother a loving smile with his big buckteeth.

Finally, looking up from the morning paper, Dad addressed Eddie flatly, "You were up until late, weren't you?"

Aaron seemed to be fine, but there was a subtle chill to both of his parents' voices, and Eddie picked up on it. It seemed like Saturday had never happened for them, and this morning was just a continuation of where they had left off Friday evening. But it didn't bother Eddie, because things were about to change.

Eddie stretched his aching body. "Yeah, a little past five, and I've barely touched the surface. I'll start again right after I finish brunch. I have a lot of work to do."

Eddie's parents exchanged puzzled glances.

Dad asked, "What exactly are you babbling on about, Eddie?"

"I was wondering when you were going to ask." From behind his back, Eddie produced a couple of books and a few sheets of notebook paper and put them on the table in front of his dad. "Bam!"

Dad examined what Eddie had put in front of him for a bit, and he cracked a wide smile.

"I suppose this is your history project."

"It sure is, pops," Eddie said enthusiastically, "and it's going to be a big one! I'm going to write about the history of African-Americans in sports. It'll have graphs and charts and everything, that is, if you'll let me use your laptop."

"Of course, I will," Dad said, his voice warming up. "That's quite an ambitious project you have there."

"And, Mom, if you can recommend any books, I'd really appreciate it," Eddie said. "All the basketball books that I own don't have too much valuable information like that."

"Maybe we can go to the bookstore later today," Mom said happily.

"Cool!"

Eddie sat down next to his brother and gave him a kind of smile that only Aaron could understand. "I've been such a fool. Don't be like me, Aaron. If you know what I mean?"

Aaron knew exactly what Eddie was talking about and nodded his head emphatically as he ate brunch eagerly. In between bites, Aaron said, "I love ya, bro!"

Setting down a plate of sausage and eggs in front of Eddie, Mom gave him a peck on the cheek. "I'm so proud of you."

"Uh, pops, mom, I know no apology in the world is gonna make up for what I did, but I'm really sorry about everything. I know I said a lot of hurtful things and did a lot of unforgiving things." Eddie could feel his heart swell up. "And I promise to hit the books hard and pursue a college education."

"That's good to hear, son." Dad looked at his older son fondly. "Let's just enjoy our brunch together and forget this whole affair ever happened. Okay?"

"Sounds like a good idea," Eddie said cheerfully, and they all ate brunch like one big happy family.

It was Monday. Fifth period had ended, and Eddie and Richie were walking to the gym together. It was indeed like old times. Yesterday, after Eddie had made headway with his report, he had gone over to Richie's home, and they had talked about comic books and video games. And they had debated about who was the best power forward in the history of basketball and agreed that it was either Karl Malone, Tim Duncan or Kevin Garnett. They had also debated about who was the most dominant center ever, and Eddie had come up with Shaquille O'Neal. But Richie had disagreed saying that it was Wilt Chamberlain, only to have Eddie say it didn't count because Richie had never seen Wilt the Stilt play.

They had talked about everything and anything, catching up on lost time, but never once did they talk about the past year or the dreadful event the other night. Yet, it was obvious to the both of them that they had an even stronger bond with each other, despite what had happened. And Eddie, in his mind, vowed to cherish Richie's friendship forever and always...

"Dawg, I tell ya. Wilt Chamberlain doesn't count!" Eddie said, still on the subject of dominant centers.

"Yeah, but nobody's ever going to score one hundred points in a game." Richie smiled. "Ever."

"But..."

At that exact moment, Eddie saw Alicia walking with her friends. She had avoided him all day, and not once did she even make eye contact. Eddie knew what the reason was, and he knew he had to make things right with her.

Richie noticed Alicia, too. "Hey, you better do something about her."

"Okay, dawg, I'll catch you later."

Eddie ran off and caught up to Alicia.

"Hey, babe! How are you doing?"

Alicia didn't even bother to turn to look at Eddie and continued to walk, leaving Eddie a few steps behind.

"I'm sorry, Alicia," Eddie screamed out.

All the other kids around them gave Eddie's strange looks, but Eddie ignored them. However, Alicia continued to walk away and Eddie gave chase.

Catching up to her again, Eddie said, "Alicia, I'm really sorry about being a jerk."

"I'm sorry, too," Alicia said coldly, deciding to finally talk. "I'm sorry about liking a jerk like you."

Eddie touched her arm. "I understand. I was wrong about a lot of things and I want to make it up to everybody."

Finally, there was eye contact. "Go on."

"The past couple of days wasn't me. I mean, it was me, but I guess it got to my head. I've done some totally retarded things, and I'm not real proud of myself right now. I'm really sorry. Give me another chance to show you the real me. Please."

Alicia smiled. She could see that Eddie was sincere. "Mr. Holder, because I do like you, I'll give you another chance. But, if you play that Jekyll and Hyde stuff on me again..."

Eddie hugged Alicia, and she let out a little squeal.

"Thank you so much, Alicia," Eddie said. "I promise I won't act like such a jerk anymore."

"You better not," Alicia warned, "if you know what's good for you."

"Don't worry, I won't." Eddie let her go. "Hey, you wanna go see a movie on Saturday or something?"

"Okay, but I have to ask my parents."

"Let me know," Eddie said. "I have things to do, but I'll call you later. Gotta go."

"Sure." Alicia smiled again. "See you tomorrow."

Eddie gave her a quick kiss on the lips and ran off to the gym.

The team was practicing lay-up drills when Eddie walked into the gym. The coach was watching his team go through the drill, while Byron Thompson was giving some pointers to Flash.

Flash saw Eddie right away but looked the other way, totally ignoring him.

Eddie just shrugged, knowing he deserved the treatment. "How's it going, Flash?"

"Good," Flash said. "Without you."

"That's enough, Flash," Byron Thompson mumbled. "Coach."

The coach turned away from the team and noticed Eddie nearby.

"Coach, I want to apologize to you and everybody," Eddie said. "Can you give me a moment, please?"

Without saying a word, the coach blew his whistle, and the guys on the court stopped their drill and gathered around Eddie. Flash and Sam stood a little behind everyone else, looking on unenthusiastically. Richie stood in front of the group, giving Eddie an encouraging look.

"Holder has something to say to all of you, ladies," the coach announced. "Holder, go ahead and make it snappy."

"The past year, and most recently, the past couple of days, I've been acting like a real pain-in-the butt. I was totally wrong," Eddie said. "I'm really, really sorry, and I'm hoping that you guys can all forgive me for being a big jerk."

Eddie continued, "Coach, Mr. Thompson, I feel so deeply ashamed. Please accept my apology. And I don't expect you to put me back on the team. I don't deserve to be reinstated."

Sam and Flash came forward.

"Did ya just use some college words?" Flash asked teasingly. "Now, I know you're back to normal!"

Eddie punched Flash in the arm lightly.

"*Hontoh ni manuke na yaroh dane*," Flash said in Japanese. "But I forgive you. You can't help it if you're an immature junior."

"You're okay, man," Sam said.

Flash, Sam and Eddie gave each other fisted fives.

"Thanks, man," Eddie said happily.

Eddie knew that it would take sometime for the wound to fully heal, but at least, for now, everything seemed to be patched up and he was satisfied.

He looked over at Richie, and Richie gave him a knowing smile.

"Sorry to interrupt this tender moment, guys," the coach said. "But, we still have a lot of practicing to do. Holder, go suit up. You're back on the team!"

"No." Eddie shook his head. "Coach, I appreciate what you're doing for me, but I can't play this season. I'm too behind in my schoolwork, and I have a lot of catching up to do. Besides, I still got one more year of high school left."

The coach looked disappointed but said anyway, "You're welcome here anytime, Holder."

"Thanks, coach," Eddie said. "And good luck in the next game. I'll be there, cheering you for you guys."

Eddie began walking out the gym, but Byron Thompson stopped him. He put his hand on Eddie's shoulder and said, "Eddie, it took a lot of guts to do what you did. You're a big man."

"Mr. Thompson, I still got my whole life ahead of me, and if it's meant to play basketball, then I'll be playing. But until then, I believe I have other priorities. Thanks for everything."

Eddie shook Byron Thompson's hand and walked out of the gym. The moment he stepped out, Eddie felt the slight cool breeze from the beach and the warmth of the sun on his cheeks, and it was just such a comfortable feeling. And it had been a long time since he felt this good.

Absorbing it all in, Eddie noticed Slamm Dunkk leaning against a wall, dribbling a basketball coolly while reading *A Christmas Carol* written by Charles Dickens. He was dressed normally in jeans and a bright red tee shirt.

"Hey, Slamm Dunkk!" Eddie greeted. "That's a great book. I can totally relate!"

Slamm Dunkk laughed a thunderous laugh.

"Thanks for showing me the way," Eddie said.

"I didn't do anything." Slamm Dunkk pointed at Eddie's heart. "You always had it in you. I just pointed you in the right direction."

"Yeah, right."

"So, what are you going to do now, Edward Holder?" Slamm Dunkk asked.

"Study my head off," Eddie replied. "I'm going to study my head off."

"Good for you," Slamm Dunkk said as both he and Eddie exchanged hi fives.

0-595-31357-4